FOUND A SECRET

SWEETFERN HARBOR MYSTERY - 23

WENDY MEADOWS

Majestic Owl Publishing LLC
P.O. Box 997
Newport, NH 03773

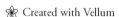 Created with Vellum

CHAPTER ONE

A llie Williams expected two guests to arrive a day earlier than the others. While waiting for them, she and Brenda Rivers chatted about the upcoming Independence Day festivities.

"The two firemen who are arriving will have their time taken up with the firefighters convention downtown," Allie said. "They probably won't be that interested in the Fourth of July stuff."

Before Brenda had time to reply, the foyer door opened. Chance Rogers walked a step ahead of his younger companion. In his early fifties, Chance was handsome and athletic, and his step didn't waver. Glen Adams looked boyish next to him, but his physique matched Chance's.

"Hello, I'm Chance Rogers. This is my fellow fireman Glen Adams. We appreciate that you accommodated us earlier than expected. We're here for the firefighters convention."

Glen stepped forward and cocked his head. "He's too serious at times. I'm here hoping to get in on some fun during the Fourth of July celebrations. I've read everything I could find about why Sweetfern Harbor is so popular at this time. I'm looking forward to a good time."

Chance shook his head. "First thing's first, Glen. I hope you can take this convention seriously so you'll learn something from it."

They bantered back and forth for a few seconds before Chance returned his attention to the women. Allie felt his eyes on her jewelry. He peered closer to get a better look at her earrings, then stepped back. Right away, as was his habit to read others, he assessed she was a studious person as well as quite artistic.

"Did you create your own jewelry?" he said.

Allie nodded. "Yes, how did you know? I find all my materials down on the beach. The earrings are from one shell, as you can see. The arrowhead sand dollar, one of my favorites." She held up her wrist. "For the bracelet, I gathered broken shells and mixed them in along with a few sand dollar pieces."

Chance appeared genuinely interested in her talent. Even Glen stepped forward to admire her creativity. Brenda was proud of her young receptionist. Allie was beginning to make a name for herself, not only for her jewelry creations, but for her paintings as well.

When the conversation turned to the Queen Anne 1890s structure, Brenda was in her element. She explained how she had inherited the Sheffield Bed and Breakfast from her uncle, Randolph Sheffield. "He spent over two years fully restoring the building to its original plans."

This brought on a new topic both men were interested in until Chance looked at his watch.

"We should move along," he said. "We have an hour and a half before the convention begins."

Brenda told them lunch would be ready in fifteen minutes. She told them where the dining room was before

Michael took their bags and started for the stairs. Chance and Glen took the heaviest bags from him, and all three ascended the winding staircase. Neither firefighter doubted their stay at the inn would be a memorable experience.

That evening, Brenda invited Phyllis and William Pendleton, Allie, and her parents, Hope and David Williams, to dine with her and Mac, her detective husband. They all enjoyed the time with their two guests, who had finished the first afternoon at the convention. Allie introduced her parents.

"My mother, Hope, owns Sweet Treats downtown, and Dad is the local news anchor on TV. You'll have to stop by and taste some of my mom's delicious goodies."

The firemen agreed they didn't want to miss it. Brenda then introduced Phyllis as her good friend and the head housekeeper at Sheffield's. "William is someone everyone relies on to bring excellent talent and entertainment into Sweetfern Harbor. He is the one who is given credit for the avalanche of tourists that come in."

"That must keep you busy, Detective," Glen said.

Mac laughed. "It does sometimes, though we look ahead to bring in nearby law enforcement when we expect larger than usual crowds. That's the way it will be this weekend, but everyone has a good time."

When dinner ended and desserts were consumed, Chance and Glen decided to take a walk along the shoreline. Phyllis and William visited a while longer, as did Hope and David. Allie had to leave early, as she had a college exam the following Monday.

"There won't be time to study this weekend," she said. "I'll see you in the morning, Brenda. We have some interesting guests coming in."

Brenda chuckled. She didn't ask for details, knowing Allie would fill her in the next day as guests checked in.

Not everyone appeared excited to have a weekend in a historic inn like the Sheffield Bed and Breakfast. Colleen Sullivan walked through the door a couple of steps ahead of her husband. At first glance, Allie decided she possessed a sour personality. Inwardly, the receptionist groaned.

"Hi, we are the Sullivans," Harry said. "I believe you have a room reserved for us?"

"Yes, welcome, you will be in Captain Scully's room, which faces the ocean. I hope you like it."

"It sounds perfect," Harry said. A quick frown in the direction of his wife disappeared almost as soon as it appeared. "I'm sure we will both enjoy the ocean air. It can be so soothing."

Allie peered closer at Colleen's face without being too intrusive. She decided the countenance held deep sadness. Brenda came from the Gathering Room and introduced herself.

"When all guests have arrived, we usually meet in the Gathering Room just across the hall from here. It's a good way to get to know a little about the people you'll be spending some of your time with throughout the weekend." She gave them an approximate time.

Harry smiled. "That's a good idea. We'll be there." Colleen didn't say a word.

After they were shown to their room, Brenda asked Allie if she noticed anything unusual about Colleen Sullivan.

"She looked very sad. I wonder if there has been a recent death in the family."

"Whatever it is, I'm sure she will speak of it if and when she wants to. In the meantime, let's make sure we work to make her stay here a pleasant one," Brenda said.

The next guest to arrive was Melissa Harris. Her eyes scanned the entire surroundings as she stopped just inside the front entrance. As she took in every detail of the structure, she introduced herself.

"I'm Melissa Harris. And what a magnificent place. Look at that mahogany staircase. I wonder how long it took to build that." There was no doubt she was more interested in taking in the encompassing view than the two women who waited with smiles on their faces for her to notice them. "I'm sorry," she said. "I suppose being a travel writer explains a little bit of my bad manners. It's just that this place takes my breath away."

"I completely understand," Allie said. She introduced herself and Brenda. "Brenda's uncle restored the Queen Anne. We all agree he did a great job of it."

Melissa focused on Brenda. "I've waited a long time to be assigned one of the coastal towns in this area. I can't believe I'm finally here."

"We can all lead you to special areas of interest while you're here," Brenda said. "Let us know when you are ready to be filled in. Every shop owner and historian in Sweetfern Harbor will be happy to talk with you."

"Thank you, Brenda, that would be wonderful. But I'm most interested in first interviewing you. This is where I want my focus to be, and then to discover what else is around here. I've heard so much about the history of the Sheffield Bed and Breakfast. I'm sure you will add things I don't know." The travel writer had obviously done her homework.

A slight flush crept into Brenda's face. She felt very pleased to know that Melissa wanted to get to know her bed and breakfast better. "I'd love to talk to you. Let me know when you wish to set up a time," Brenda said.

After she left for her room, Allie beamed. "That will be great, Brenda. It's another way to get your name out there." Brenda agreed. Each year, word spread further about the Sheffield Bed and Breakfast. Many interested people knew

Randolph when he was in theater before settling in Sweetfern Harbor.

The energy swept Allie and Brenda when the next couple entered. Holly and Luke Parker walked at a clip, but not before both were drawn to the ceilings and walls of the inn. The paintings that lined the passageway caught Holly's eye. "I can't help but notice those beautiful paintings. I've heard about the famous boat race each year. Are those true depictions?"

Brenda joined her. "Yes, there were three very famous captains who competed against one another. That was a while back. We still have the race, but there are three new competitors now who have built up quite a reputation of their own. Usually, that competition is closer to the end of summer. I can give you a schedule if you're interested in returning for it."

"It is fascinating, I'm sure." Holly bent her head slightly. "I'm a museum curator. Paintings of this quality never fail to catch my eye." She accepted Brenda's offer of a schedule.

Luke chatted with Allie while his wife discussed the paintings with Brenda. "How interesting that you're a musician," Allie said. "What kind of music do you play?"

"I'm a mere jazz entertainer." His eyes twinkled, but Allie wasn't sure if he put himself down on purpose or was teasing her. She was saved by his wife.

"He is a professional jazz musician, Allie. Don't let him fool you into thinking otherwise. He has quite a following, not only around New York but areas of Europe, too. He plays the saxophone."

"You must give us the pleasure of hearing you play," Brenda said. She mentioned the enclosed veranda. "It is very conducive to music since, in the reconstruction, Randolph made sure it was readied for musicians. The walls are fabric acoustic panels, though you'd never know it by looking at the room. Once the doors are closed, it is also soundproof."

"I'm stunned that he was so forward thinking while retaining the historic ambience," Luke said.

"We use that room for many of our events for a variety of reasons." Brenda mentioned a Casino Night fundraiser they had once as well as wedding receptions. "On occasion, we've had small orchestras entertain, especially during wintertime. Usually, they are fundraisers for charities."

"There will be so much to take in right here," Holly said, "though we have come to celebrate Independence Day."

"Perhaps we should plan on staying longer than originally planned," Luke said. "I don't see how we're going to do everything in three short days." His wife reminded him of responsibilities in their careers that waited for them.

"Plan on returning," Allie said. "We have many repeat guests. No one can take in everything with just one visit here."

All agreed. Brenda told them about meeting in the Gathering Room if they wished. They promised they'd be back down. Brenda and Phyllis were pleased to see all guests opted to meet to get acquainted. Colleen and Harry Sullivan entered the room last. Colleen remained stoic. Harry stayed by her side as they made their way around the room. Melissa overheard Harry state their occupations.

"I'm a concrete truck driver for a large construction company. Colleen works at a loan company as their receptionist. We had the opportunity to come this direction and took advantage of it." Melissa failed to divert her eyes from the despondent woman. She decided to befriend her. Melissa gently touched Colleen's arm and motioned her aside.

"Is there something bothering you? I'll be glad to help if I can." At first, Colleen withdrew. Melissa hoped she hadn't overstepped her place. After all, she didn't know Colleen Sullivan at all.

"I see you didn't get a drink yet," Melissa said. "What do you like? There is tea, coffee, wine, and other cold beverages."

"I'll take a Diet Coke, thanks," Colleen said. She wanted to confide in someone, but not yet.

CHAPTER TWO

The first evening of dinner began. After all guests had arrived, Brenda introduced Mac. "A few of you have met my husband already. Mac is head detective of our local police department and quite busy with his work. That's not to say that if you need anything while here, he won't have time to assist you, as we all will."

Mac stood up. "I do keep busy, but as guests, you are our priority here. Welcome to all of you, and we hope you enjoy your stay with us."

A few of the guests found it novel to have an inn owner also a police detective, but Brenda never wanted to announce she was also a law officer. Her focus was on her B&B. She had agreed to be inducted by Chief Bob Ingram only if he promised to use her for isolated cases. Brenda's background included being assistant to a private detective in Michigan before she found herself in Sweetfern Harbor and later married to Detective Mac Rivers. Chief Ingram had recognized her astuteness in getting below the surface of details when it came to solving crimes.

When dinner ended, most guests decided to walk

downtown. Shops stayed open later in summertime, especially when special events were going on in town. Colleen Sullivan told her husband she wanted to invite Melissa Harris to walk with her.

"I'm not sure you will enjoy tagging along with me anyway, Harry," she said. "You always complain that I take too long in stores."

"It's fine with me," Harry said. "I've heard there is a shop that specializes in antique guns and ammunition. I might go check it out."

Colleen grimaced. She didn't like her husband's obsession with firearms, whether they were modern or antique, but she kept silent about it for the moment. "We'll meet up later," she said. "I'll call you when Melissa and I are ready to turn in for the night back at the B&B." Harry agreed. He was anxious to be on his own for a while.

Melissa was happy to go with Colleen. Melissa's curiosity knew no bounds, and she hoped her new acquaintance would tell her about her worries. "Brenda told me that her daughter owns Jenny's Blossoms. She sells flowers and local handmade crafts. Do you want to start there?"

Colleen agreed. "I heard someone say that Brenda and Mac have been married for only a few years. I believe Jenny is actually her stepdaughter."

This was the most animation Melissa had seen in Colleen. Just as suddenly as the burst of conversation, Colleen retreated into her shell. Thoughts ran through Melissa's mind. Should she urge Colleen to spill it all or try to be patient? She didn't have to consider any approach. Colleen spoke as soon as they left the gates of the Sheffield Bed and Breakfast.

"I don't know you well at all, Melissa, but there is something about you that makes me want to tell you about something very grave on my mind." She slowed her pace, and Melissa kept alongside her. "I'm here in Sweetfern Harbor for one reason and one only. Harry agreed to come with me, but he usually stands on the sideline of my issue. I hope I can trust you."

Melissa touched her arm. "Of course, you can trust me, Colleen. I won't breathe a word of whatever you tell me."

"I am here to find my long-lost sister, Marcy Scott. She has been missing for a very long time." Colleen stopped. "My parents have done very little, if anything, to find her. I didn't even know about her until recent years. I always yearned for a sister. When I saw her picture online, I knew for sure right away that that person was my sister."

Melissa felt confused. "Why didn't your parents look for her?"

"They both wanted to act as if she never existed at all. When I asked them why they hadn't told me about her, at first, my mother laughed as if I was joking. Then she denied I ever had a sister. The photo I saw looked a lot like me and specifically identified her as Marcy Scott. That was my last name before I married Harry. My parents are hiding a deep, dark secret."

"How did you trace her to Sweetfern Harbor?"

"I didn't trace her specifically to this town. I learned she lived somewhere along the seaboard in this region. I decided to begin here. I admit, when I saw ads about the weekend July Fourth celebrations, I used it to lure Harry to come along with me."

"You must tell the detective. He could put a search warrant out for her or something. I'm not sure of the procedure, but he seems like he is someone who would pay attention."

Colleen vigorously shook her head. "No. No one must know. If word gets out to the law, she may disappear again. I have no idea what she has been through, but the less trauma for her, the better."

Melissa had no words. Who wouldn't want every resource to find someone close to you? She asked Colleen if law enforcement anywhere had ever been contacted.

"Early on, I took the photo and story to the local police department in my hometown. When my father found out what I had done, he met with the chief of police and told him I had no missing sister. My father has clout in Dunmore —that's in Pennsylvania, by the way—because he is on the city council and has close ties with all segments of the workings of the town. They listened to him and didn't look for her at all."

Colleen's eyes misted as she continued the story. "I took it to another police department outside Dunmore. The chief of police there seemed very concerned at first. He worked with me on details. They put out flyers trying to find Marcy. After a few weeks, they didn't push further—I think it's because they found out I'd never even met her, and no one who knows her has filed a missing persons report. So no, it's pointless going to the police. If I could afford one, I'd hire a private detective."

Melissa shook her head, her brow furrowed. She was certain that this search for Marcy Scott would prove fruitless. Colleen Sullivan didn't seem to have the resources it would take to find her sister. She voiced her concerns to Colleen.

"I've learned a lot, Melissa. I've gone online and word is spreading. I've even received positive responses. More than one led me to this region." She stopped walking again. Melissa followed suit. "I picked you to tell this story to, Melissa, because you are a travel writer. You must have met many people in your work from across the country. I have a photo of Marcy to show you." She dug in her bag and retrieved the picture. "I know it's a long shot, but have you ever met this woman in your travels?"

Melissa took the photo and scrutinized it. "I've met many people, as you say, but she doesn't look familiar to me." She tilted the photo for a better look. Melissa shook her head. "I'm sorry, I don't recognize her at all. I do see faint resemblances to you in her." Melissa had to look again to discover any similarities at all. The eyes were formed in the same manner as Colleen's. The complexion resembled hers. She could be her sister, but there wasn't much to go on.

"I don't wish to push the matter of involving local police," Melissa said. "Not only is Mac the head detective at the precinct here, but I overheard someone say Brenda is also a law officer. I'm sure both would be concerned enough to look into the disappearance with great care. Why not tell them so you could move faster in your search?"

Colleen's eyes grew steely. "I told you I don't trust the police." She'd had no idea that both innkeepers were bona fide police officers when she booked her stay. "I can't take more rejection when they ultimately brush me off." She picked up her pace.

They were in front of Jenny's Blossoms. Melissa received the message that there was no point in pursuing the subject. Inside the shop, Jenny Jones greeted them with a smile. Melissa told her she was interested in local craft items. Colleen moved to the display of flowers behind glass. She admired the beauty while Jenny told Melissa which inhabitant of Sweetfern Harbor crafted each item. The door to the shop opened, and Colleen looked around to face a young police officer. He approached Jenny and kissed her lightly.

"This is my husband, Detective Bryce Jones," Jenny said. She looked at Bryce. "Aren't you taking your break a little early today?"

"I couldn't wait to see you." His startling blue eyes flirted with his wife. "After this visit, I'll stop to see Nicholas. I feel it's a good thing to check up on him. Surprise visits are good."

Jenny laughed. "You know he is well taken care of, but both of you will be happy to see one another." Jenny turned to her two customers. "Nicholas is our toddler son. I bring him down here sometimes, but lately he's become too active. I don't want him distracting me or the customers."

"I'm sure he is precious," Melissa said. "It fascinates me to know that the owners of the Sheffield Bed and Breakfast have law careers, plus their son-in-law, too. Does it run any farther in the family?"

"As far as we know, it's the three of them," Jenny said. Bryce kissed his wife on the cheek and waved goodbye.

Colleen turned back to admire the flower displays. Confiding in Melissa could have been a mistake, she thought. She must do everything in her power to keep from bringing up the subject of Marcy again with her.

Melissa purchased some jewelry made by the B&B's receptionist—a matching necklace and bracelet. "I love the shells that Allie chose. She is very talented." Jenny agreed. When the women were back outside, Colleen told Melissa she had lost interest in more shopping.

"I understand, Colleen. You have a lot on your mind right now. I'll walk back with you. I'd like to take an evening stroll along the beach."

Brenda noticed the two women when they walked into the foyer. The outing hadn't seemed to change the dejected countenance of Colleen. Melissa chattered along with no response.

"Did you two enjoy our coastal village?" Brenda said.

"It is so lovely. We got into Jenny's shop in time to browse. I think she was getting ready to close soon after we left. Her husband, Bryce, stopped by." Melissa smiled. "I think he must be on night duty tonight. He told Jenny he was going to check on their young son before his break was over."

"I'm glad you met him. He and Jenny are very devoted to Nicholas. We enjoy every minute we get with him, too," Brenda said. She watched Colleen walk toward the stairs. "Do you need anything, Colleen?" She shook her head no without looking back.

Melissa met Brenda's eyes. She wanted to tell her what was going on with Colleen, but she hadn't forgotten her promise.

Colleen knew Melissa's intentions were out of her hands now. What if she broke her promise and told Brenda? She was accustomed to very little interest in her missing sister by law enforcement.

Something about the look on Melissa's face told Brenda she wanted to say something but held back. "It appeared you were trying to cheer Colleen up. Is she all right? I hope the two of you enjoyed your stroll."

"We did enjoy it. She felt compelled to confide in me regarding a concern of hers. It has nothing to do with your bed and breakfast, Brenda. I hope I helped her in some way, but we'll see." Melissa felt it was time to change the subject. "I bought this necklace and bracelet from Jenny. She told me Allie made them."

Brenda peered at them. "She is very artistic. She will be happy to know you bought some of her jewelry. She also paints and has sold some of her paintings downtown."

A few minutes passed in light conversation. Brenda asked if her guest needed anything. "I can't think of a thing. I'm going to take a stroll down by the ocean," Melissa said. "It will be a short one since I'm almost ready to turn in."

They said goodnight. Brenda walked down the

passageway to the back door. Chef Pierre had finished for the night. Brenda stopped in the kitchen to grab some herbal tea bags. Then she headed for the cottage.

She thought about Melissa's words. She hoped that whatever was on Colleen's mind, it would be resolved after a relaxing few days. The ocean air alone continually soothed Brenda when she worried about anything. Her pace picked up when she saw Mac's car in the driveway. Entering into their living room, she was greeted with a whiff of fresh coffee. Mac came from the kitchen and kissed her.

"I have a hot cup of fresh coffee for you, Brenda. Don't worry, it's decaf. I didn't think you'd want to be up all night." He chuckled. "I stopped at Sweet Treats before coming home. Hope sneaked me inside before closing." He produced some petit fours, a favorite of Brenda's.

Words weren't needed between them. Contentment settled in knowing that when she married Detective Mac Rivers, she married the best.

CHAPTER THREE

Everyone was up early the next morning. Brenda entered the dining room to greet her guests. Brenda noticed that since arriving, the two firefighters rarely sat apart from one another. She understood, since they had so much in common with one another. Each one showed interest in their table companions, however.

"I thought about you two last night," Holly Parker said. "We have some unique firefighter artifacts in the museum where I work. I have some photos of them on my phone that I thought you'd like to see."

Chance told her that he was very interested. Glen Adams got up from his chair to take a look over Holly's shoulder.

"This is an early 1800s fire hat," Holly said. "It's decorated depicting a particular fire station." She moved to the next one. "This is my favorite. In the 1800s through early 1900s, every home had a fire bucket. Each family engraved the family name on theirs to make sure the bucket was returned to them."

Chance and Glen delved into the conversation as she showed more photos. "I envy you your job," Chance said.

"These items make me glad I'm fighting fires in a more modern way."

Luke Parker sat with the Sullivans. "What do the two of you do?"

"Colleen is a receptionist for a loan company," Harry replied. "I drive a concrete truck for a construction company in Scranton, Pennsylvania."

"Oh, right. I apologize," Luke said. "I did hear you tell someone that last night. When I was in high school, my father took me to a construction site to inform me that construction workers were more important than musicians. I agreed they were important, but I had a place, too. After that, he gave up on me." Luke chuckled. "I don't think he agrees with my choice even to this day."

"I do enjoy my work," Harry said, "but my real interest is delving into unsolved crimes. At least, in my head I do that. I'd love to be a private investigator or detective. Crime solving is something that sharpens the mind."

Brenda overheard him. "Why not study the field while you work your day job? You could also assist in breaking cases. There are too many cold cases out there."

Harry smiled. "I've thought about that. Maybe I will look into it."

Chance and Glen stood up. "We have a few final hours at the convention this morning," Chance said. "Then by noon, we'll be free to start enjoying the celebrations set for today. I'm sure Glen is happy about that."

Glen chuckled. "I am. The convention has been interesting, but I'm ready to have some fun."

Soon the other guests scattered. Melissa caught up with Colleen and Harry when they walked in the direction of the ocean.

"Colleen, I'd like to ask a few more questions about our discussion yesterday. If you don't mind, that is."

"Harry knows all about it. Feel free to ask."

"I'd like a deeper description of Marcy. Did you read up on any of her interests, or her occupation? If she is in or near Sweetfern Harbor, she would be easier to spot if we had an idea of where she would go."

Colleen thought for a moment. "As you saw from the photo, she strongly resembles me. The website I found her on shows no way to directly contact her. Believe me, I've searched more than once for direct contact information. All I have is her photo. No idea of what kind of person she is or what she likes to do."

Melissa decided to press her. "Think hard, Colleen. What did it say about her?" Harry's lips thinned, but Melissa continued. "What were the circumstances of her disappearance? I know your parents haven't been helpful, but did you discover anything more about her online?"

"I don't wish to discuss this further, Melissa. We are going to enjoy the ocean."

Melissa got the point. As she turned to go back to the B&B, she caught the frown and penetrating eyes of Harry on her. Melissa felt sure the look was one of a warning.

Before she was out of earshot, Melissa heard Harry's harsh voice directed at his wife. His tone sounded threatening, but she couldn't make out the words.

More than ever, Melissa wanted to talk things over with Brenda. Then she recalled her promise. How many times had she promised interviewees she'd not write certain things revealed about them? A promise was a promise.

Chance Rogers and Glen Adams were happy when the convention finally ended. They didn't stay for acclamations and awards. It was almost time for the parade to begin. Luke Parker stood outside the Morning Sun Coffee Shop. He had his saxophone with him.

"Isn't that a little bulky to be carrying around?" Glen asked him.

Luke laughed. "I've been playing to entertain the tourists. I have my case with me. Once I get inside the coffee shop, I'll tuck it away."

Molly Lindsay smiled her welcome when they approached the counter.

"I heard someone famous was out there on the sidewalk entertaining," she said. "I'm Molly Lindsay and a big fan of yours, Mr. Parker."

"Please, everyone calls me Luke, especially my fans." He eyed the young woman. "You look like someone I've met somewhere."

"Are you staying at the Sheffield Bed and Breakfast?" Molly said.

"We are."

"I'm Phyllis's daughter. She's the head housekeeper there. Everyone says we resemble one another."

After they all sat with their coffees, Luke said, "I'd like to see those floats before the parade. Mac told me they will line up down at Wally's Boat Shop. Wally Doyle builds most of the boats we'll see around here. When it comes to celebrations in town and floats needed, he makes room for contestants to build theirs in his warehouse."

"I'm game," Glen said. "We won't get that close a look during the parade."

"This town is bubbling over with talent," Chance said. "I'd like to see what they've come up with."

When Wally discovered the three men were guests at the B&B, he said, "Come with me. I'll show you their float. It's spectacular this year. Allie Williams had great ideas for it."

The float was more than expected. An exact replica of the inn had been erected in the middle of the float. All agreed it would stand out in the parade. Glen was the first to notice

Allie at a long table in the back corner. She had enlisted helpers, and all were rolling sheets of paper around wrapped candy.

"What are you doing?" Luke asked.

"The papers have a brief history of Sheffield's on them," Allie said. "The taffy sticks are wrapped in wax paper and we're inserting them in the rolled paper."

"That's a great idea," Chance said.

Allie laughed. "I have a dual purpose here. Fans along the route will get a taste of my mother's taffy from Sweet Treats, along with the history of the bed and breakfast." She pointed to the float. "Jenny's Blossoms provided the red, white, and blue carnations. This year, she decided to join us rather than enter a float representing her shop."

They admired the rest of the floats before they left to get choice spots along the route. Luke called Holly. She told him she had joined Melissa and some townspeople they met. "I'll meet you later at the coffee shop. That is, if we can get in the door. It's quite a popular place in town."

Luke agreed they would meet there. Floats began lining up. Brenda, Phyllis, and Allie got onto theirs. Other staff members joined them. The crowds cheered as the floats began parading down the street. Guests, plus many others, cheered loudly when the Sheffield Bed and Breakfast float passed by. Children and adults alike scrambled for the wrapped taffies. Luke noticed several tucked the paper with the history on it into their pockets or purses. The fans on the sidelines increased.

"It's hard to believe that a small town like this one attracts crowds like this," Glen said.

"The town has someone who brings people in. Phyllis Pendleton's husband," Chance said. "His name is William. It seems he knows many people in the entertainment circles. He's the one who put the town on the map."

When the last float and band passed by, the crowds began to disperse. Luke, Chance, and Glen headed back to the coffee shop to meet up with Melissa and Holly.

"Isn't that saxophone getting heavy?" Glen said.

"I'm used to lugging it around. I may play a little more on the street. If the crowd gets bored, I'll take it back to the B&B and unload it," Luke said.

Melissa and Holly talked about the unusual floats. "The bands were great, too," Holly said. "I love parades." When they saw the men, they waved.

Melissa looked around the dispersing crowd. "Did you see Colleen and Harry during the parade?" she asked Holly.

"I wasn't looking for them, but I don't recall seeing them. Of course, they could have been swallowed up in the crowd."

Melissa took one last look around before she recalled the sinister look Harry had thrown her. It remained a mystery to her as to why neither of them wanted to give more details about Colleen's missing sister. How did either of them expect to find her on their own? This might prove to be the one time that Melissa broke a promise.

Customers in the coffee shop were delighted to spot Luke Parker.

"Are you going to play again on the street, Luke?" a woman asked.

"I'll play as long as I don't bore everyone. What do you like to hear?"

The woman in her mid-forties beamed. "I had no idea you'd ask for requests. I have always loved listening to Dizzy Gillespie's 'A Night in Tunisia.'"

"Done," Luke said.

"How about 'Ain't Misbehavin'' by Fats Waller?" someone shouted.

More people called out jazz tunes until Luke stood up.

He put up both hands to stop them. "I get it. You want to hear jazz. Come on, let's go outside."

He started with "A Night in Tunisia" and from there he played almost every request until he signaled for a pause. "I can see you aren't tired of my playing, and I appreciate that, but it's time for me to give this instrument a rest."

The crowd stepped back and applauded again while he packed the saxophone into its case.

"I've never heard anyone play like you did," Chance said. "I can see why you are so successful. Your father should be proud of you now."

"I don't know about that. He doesn't say much about my music even now."

Molly couldn't believe how much Luke Parker did to increase her business. Brenda and Phyllis had stopped to listen to Luke before going into the Morning Sun Coffee Shop.

"Who won the prize for best float?" Molly asked them.

"We haven't heard yet," Phyllis said. "They should have results out soon."

Molly set the espresso and latté down in front of her mother and Brenda. Brenda watched Colleen and Harry Sullivan walk into the coffee shop. Brenda waved to them, but neither saw her. There was one empty bistro table left in the corner of the shop, where they sat down. Only a table for two separated Brenda and Phyllis from the Sullivans. The din in the shop overrode their voices. Brenda watched as they bent their heads toward one another. They sat back when their drinks arrived, then resumed positions. Colleen's voice rose over the noise.

"I have to find her, Harry. It means everything to me. You know that."

Harry stood up and threw his napkin on the table. He stalked from the shop but not before he noticed Brenda and

Phyllis. He managed to produce a weak smile and left. Brenda turned to Colleen and invited her to sit with them. She declined and then followed her husband onto the street.

"What was that all about?" Phyllis said.

"I'm not sure," Brenda said.

CHAPTER FOUR

P hyllis and Brenda were leaving the coffee shop when Molly called them back in.

"They're announcing the float winners now. You may want to head back that way. Everyone is gathering at the grandstand."

Phyllis and Brenda hurried to the spot just as their float was named winner. One of the judges handed Brenda the coveted trophy and congratulations. When she turned toward the applause, Brenda was surprised to see how many people were there. She waved the trophy and thanked the judges.

Molly told Melissa that Brenda and Phyllis left to find out who won the prize for best float. She saw Brenda waving the trophy in the air and heard the crowds shout their approval. Maybe now wasn't the time to break her promise. She didn't want to spoil the pride in Brenda's eyes. She watched Allie join her and Phyllis. Brenda stated to everyone it was Allie Williams who gave the artistic touch to the float. Everyone cheered again. Allie beamed.

"This is one more trophy to add to the showroom at the museum," Brenda said.

It was custom that winners displayed their trophies in the local museum. Brenda decided to hold onto hers until everyone at the B&B had a chance to get a good look at it.

"Brenda," Melissa said. "I hate to interrupt your time of elation, but I have something I must speak with you about." Melissa hung her head briefly. "I'm sorry. I didn't even congratulate you. I'm so happy the best float was yours."

"Thank you. It belongs to all of us at the Sheffield Bed and Breakfast. What did you wish to speak about?"

"Is law enforcement in Sweetfern Harbor aware of a missing woman by the name of Marcy Scott?"

"I don't recall that name. Why do you ask?"

Conflicting thoughts fought inside Melissa's head. She had come this far, and there was no turning back now. "Colleen confided in me. I promised not to involve the police, but she is desperate to find her sister. I hate breaking my promise to her, but there is no way she will find her without help." Consternation flooded her face. "I hope I'm doing the right thing."

"Is this Marcy Scott her sister then?" Melissa nodded. "I'll ask Mac about it."

"I don't have any details. Either Colleen didn't want to give them to me, or she doesn't know details. She only has a photo of her sister." Melissa told Brenda everything she knew about the case.

"Why didn't she go to the police?"

Melissa explained Colleen's distrust of the law. "She made me promise not to tell you or Mac. She can never know I told you about it. I'm hoping it can be looked into without involving me."

"I promise she won't know for now." Brenda looked hard

at Melissa and determined she told the truth of what she knew. "I'll ask Mac about it. He's been around Sweetfern Harbor his entire life. He may have heard of her. He may even have a cold case file on her."

Mac approached his wife to congratulate her. "I had a feeling our float would come in first, Brenda. Everyone made that happen." Brenda presented him with the trophy.

"I'll take it to the museum tomorrow morning. For the rest of this day, everyone at the bed and breakfast should enjoy it." Mac's eyebrows rose when he noticed his wife's demeanor change from joy to concern. "Have you heard about a missing woman named Marcy Scott?"

Mac looked alarmed. "Did someone go missing today?"

"No, no, it is someone who has been missing for quite some time, although I'm not sure for how long. She is Colleen Sullivan's sister. Her name is Marcy Scott. Colleen is in the area to find her. It seems she got a lead about her whereabouts from someone online and is determined to find her."

"Why didn't she tell us to begin with? We have plenty of resources to find missing persons," Mac said. "I'm not saying we're always successful, but she could have everything she needs to find her sister. Have her come down and give me details."

Brenda told Mac why that couldn't happen. Melissa silently crossed her fingers behind her back, hoping the detective wouldn't insist on talking with Colleen. Mac glanced in Melissa's direction.

"Okay, I'll keep it mum for now. It could be one of the cold cases, but I don't recall that name at all."

Mac told them he'd go and look at files now. Melissa thanked them for their interest. She liked Brenda and Mac and felt sure they would keep her secret. She spotted Holly and Luke. When she joined them, they were getting ready to go back to the bed and breakfast.

"I loved your music, Luke. You know how to make that saxophone talk, don't you?"

Luke laughed and thanked her. "I love playing. As for Holly, I'm thankful she puts up with me."

Holly rolled her eyes. "I try." She asked Melissa if she'd like to join them for the walk back.

"I think I will. I'm ready to enjoy the salty air again. Isn't it wonderful to have the Atlantic Ocean so close to the B&B?"

"I want to explore the Queen Anne structure more," Holly said. "Brenda promised a tour for anyone interested. I hope she comes home soon so I can ask her."

"She will be here soon. Sheffield's float won first place. She's bringing the trophy back in a little while."

"I'm going to stretch out on that comfortable bed," Luke said. "I'm ready for a nap."

When Colleen and Harry left the coffee shop, it proved impossible for Colleen to keep up with her husband. She finally allowed him his space, knowing she had upset him once again. Colleen stopped in front of the My Heart Bridal Shop. The dresses in the window reminded her of how happy she had been shopping for her own bridal gown. She'd had a limited budget but found a dress that fit her perfectly. She smiled when she recalled the pleasure on Harry's face when she walked down the aisle of the little country church in rural Dunmore. It seemed so long ago now. The longer they remained together, the less he took pleasure in anything about her or her interests.

Colleen meandered along and stopped in front of a shop that sold theatrical attire. A lady was in the window adjusting a medieval costume for display. The lady, Maggie Johnson according to the name tag on her blouse, waved at her. The gesture brought a smile to Colleen's face. She had barely made time to enjoy the people in the town. There were shops she wanted to visit but she hadn't allowed time for that, either.

Colleen's thoughts wandered. The closer she got to the bed and breakfast, the stronger the calming sea air hit her. She took the steps down to the beach. Kicking off her flip-flops, she relished the feel of the sand between her toes. In the distance, two boats cruised near the shore. She heard a man in Wright's Boat Rental shout to someone. The man in the motorboat shouted back and moved on. Colleen squished her toes deeper into the sand. People on the beach smiled at her when she passed them by. When the sand turned to pebbles, then rocks, she put her shoes back on. The flat rock ahead of her served as a place to sit and enjoy the view.

Her thoughts reverted to her parents. She remembered the day when she asked her mother for the first time why she didn't have a sibling. Her mother's pat answer was always "You are enough for us."

Was she enough? She never felt she measured up. Her mother had gone on to say that if they had had more children, she wouldn't have received the attention she was given. "We would have had to divide that attention from you to make room for a sibling." Despite her mother's answers, Colleen felt incomplete without a sibling, especially a sister.

Five years ago, Colleen received an invitation to a class reunion. She hadn't kept in touch with her once best friend, Sara Turner. She wondered if Sara would attend the reunion. That was the incentive to pull out her old yearbook. She looked for Sara, who was just as Colleen remembered. Then she thumbed through pages of upper classmates she barely knew at all. She stopped on the photo that caught her eye. The young woman on the senior page looked like her. She even had the same last name as her. That was the day she spent an inordinate amount of time studying the photo of Marcy Scott.

Colleen had spent two years in college before dropping out. She had barely spoken with her parents since the day she ended her first year. Looking at the yearbook photo, she knew she had to ask them about it. She gathered the book, and, with her hand to mark the page, she called her mother.

"Who is Marcy Scott?" she asked.

"Is this Colleen? We haven't heard from you for quite a while."

"Of course it's me. I wouldn't be calling now if it wasn't so important that I'm forced to do so. Who is Marcy Scott?"

"I don't know that name. Is she a relative?" Ruth Scott said.

"I'm asking you. She looks just like me. Is she my sister you've never told me about?"

Silence was the answer. After a few seconds, Ruth regained her composure. "Colleen, you've never had a sister. I don't know who you are looking at, but she isn't your sister."

Colleen slammed the phone down on the table when she ended the call. She opened her laptop and put in the name Marcy Scott. After fifteen minutes, the photo came up. The woman looked a little older, but, other than that, Colleen was convinced that she strongly resembled her. The last name remained the same, which told her that her sister hadn't married. She was so convinced that this Marcy Scott was her sister she began researching every site she could think of. She took one more chance to pin her mother down to who the person was. She took the photo she had downloaded from the website along with the yearbook to her parents' house. They looked surprised to see her walk in when her mother opened the door. Daniel Scott smiled at his daughter and asked how she had been.

Ruth Scott noticed the photo and yearbook in her daughter's hands. She dreaded the next conversation, knowing it would end in an argument.

"I want you both to look at the photo in the yearbook and this more recent photo. Her name is Marcy Scott. You will notice she looks exactly like me. Will you once and for all admit she is my sister?"

Ruth and Daniel looked at one another. Daniel spoke. "Colleen, your mother has already told you that you've never had a sibling. I admit there are similarities here, but we do not know anyone named Marcy Scott. You must know that Scott is not an unusual last name. She could be anyone."

"I should have expected you to deny it all. I'll just have to go my own way and find out for myself." Colleen had gathered her evidence and flounced across the room to the door. Colleen vowed from that moment forward to not speak to her parents about the matter again. From now on, she would go on her own and find her sister. She soon realized she was looking for a needle in a haystack and she confided in her husband. Harry showed immediate interest and he agreed the woman in the photo looked like his wife. "She could be your sister, but if your parents are telling you they didn't have another child, how could she be?"

"They're lying."

Colleen almost gave up when she kept meeting dead ends. Even the police blew her off when she had no proof that she was the sister of a missing person. A year passed, and then she spotted an article about Marcy Scott. The article stated a woman named Marcy Scott of Black Mountain, Pennsylvania had gone missing for two years. It had become a cold case with no new leads. When she reached out to her growing fan base on a missing persons website, several people who lived along the Eastern Seaboard told her they had seen Marcy in the region. Colleen convinced Harry to take a weekend trip to Sweetfern Harbor.

"I have to start somewhere. I need your support, Harry."

Harry finally agreed when he discovered everything the town and seaside offered.

CHAPTER FIVE

Most guests returned to the town to enjoy the afternoon music and festivities. Several food trucks had been licensed to sell along the side streets. The two firemen enjoyed hamburgers from one of them. They sat down to eat at one of the tables set up near the food truck.

"I'm sure glad that convention is over with," Glen said. "It's time we had some fun."

Chance returned the comments with a brief frown. "You know that we have to learn from them. I thought the presentations were better than usual this year." He decided to let the subject go and he waved Holly and Luke over.

"I see you left your saxophone at home this time," Chance said. "I suppose constantly playing for free isn't a good move for you." He chuckled.

"I don't usually play this much unless in front of paying audiences, but I really liked entertaining on the streets."

Holly saw Melissa and called to her to join them. As soon as she sat down, Melissa began to scan others around them.

More than once, her new friends wondered who she was looking for. Her eyes continually moved around the throng of people enjoying the festivities.

"Are you looking for someone in particular?" Glen said.

A faint tint of pink clouded Melissa's face. Options fought against one another in her brain. What harm if she involved more people in the search for Colleen's missing sister?

"I will tell you something that each of you must swear to keep confidential." The others leaned in closer. All promised to keep her secret. "Colleen Sullivan has reason to look so worried and glum," Melissa said. "She is here to find her missing sister. It seems someone told her that Marcy Scott has been seen along this region of the seaboard."

"Surely, the police are on top of it," Holly said.

Melissa shook her head. "That's part of the secret of it all. She is adamant about not involving the law." Melissa explained Colleen's reasons.

Everyone sat silently, mulling over her news. Glen spoke first. "How long has this sister been missing?"

"She just found out in recent years that she even had a sister. She found her in an old yearbook when she was looking up a friend to get in touch with again. Her sister is older than she is. The school she attended was quite large. She had no idea of anyone with the same last name as hers. Before her marriage to Harry, her last name was Scott."

"Do you have a copy of the photo?" Holly said.

"Colleen has one and showed it to me. I must admit the young woman resembled Colleen when they were in high school. She found another one online when she began her search. She swears the resemblance is still there." Melissa paused. "If you want to help, start looking around for someone that looks like Colleen. Above all, do not tell anyone else about this."

"You should tell Brenda and Mac about this, Melissa," Glen said. "You could ask them to keep it low-key."

Melissa bent her head. "I admit that I already mentioned it to them. They agreed to keep it out of the public eye for now anyway. I hope I did the right thing, but Colleen is so upset about it all. There is no way she can find Marcy on her own."

"I am beginning to like the idea of solving a mystery," Chance said. "Mystery novels are favorites of mine."

The group decided to spread out when they finished eating. While they enjoyed the wares along the street and the music and antics of street entertainers, they each kept an eye out for people who resembled Colleen Sullivan.

Colleen and Harry stood waiting for cold drinks. Colleen's eyes darted around the crowd of people nearby. Harry nudged his wife and motioned for her to sit with him. Beneath the large white cedar tree was a bench. Colleen felt weary and took advantage of the break. Harry glanced at her. Her taut face hadn't relaxed since their arrival.

"Colleen, you need to give yourself time to enjoy our surroundings. Any other time, you would have been completely caught up in celebrations like these. Give it up for now."

Colleen's head jerked to face him. "How can I give up so easily? Wouldn't you want to do everything in your power to find a brother you never knew you had? And to find out he has been missing for two years as well? What would you do, Harry?"

"I would work with the police if I was sure he was my brother. You have no proof you even have a sister, much less one that is missing. You are too involved in things that aren't even certain."

Harry often wanted to tell his wife that he once called her parents and questioned them thoroughly. They came across as sincere people who were very worried about their daughter and her obsession. Now was not the time to reveal he had gone behind her back. Her lack of mental stability increased with the intensity. Harry had no reason to believe Colleen didn't have a normal upbringing. He didn't understand why she was so consumed with finding her phantom sister.

"I'm ready to enjoy myself down on the beach, Colleen. The salt air and cool breezes will do both of us good. Let's go."

Colleen shook her head. "You go on, Harry. I'm going to stick around down here awhile longer."

Harry glanced at his watch and then looked at the sky. The afternoon sun ebbed. Sunset would soon follow, and then the fireworks and night-long dancing. "I'll meet up with you again at the bed and breakfast. We don't want to miss the fireworks later this evening." He recalled how much fun Colleen had been during celebrations of any kind. He reminded her of the dancing. "You always loved to dance, Colleen. Let's spend the night dancing after the fireworks."

Colleen barely recalled enjoying dancing. "I may do that if my heart is in it, Harry."

Her husband attempted to hold his temper. He turned from her and deposited the empty cup in the bin and left on his own. Glen Adams caught up with Harry, who was in no mood for company.

"Leaving so soon, Harry?"

"I need some time alone. I'll see you at dinner." Harry felt guilt arise within him at leaving his wife. He swallowed. "Are you planning to enjoy the fireworks?"

"I'm not missing anything," Glen said. "I'm hoping I can persuade Melissa to spend the night dancing with me." He winked at Harry. Harry smiled and told him he'd see him later.

That evening, everyone had returned to Sheffield Bed and Breakfast for dinner. Each guest seemed to have a story to tell about the events going on around Sweetfern Harbor. No one planned to miss the fireworks. Even Colleen and Harry appeared more relaxed with one another.

"Are there more celebrations scheduled around town for tomorrow?" Melissa said.

"There will be a pancake breakfast for anyone who wishes to go," Brenda said. "It starts at seven, and I believe will continue until around ten o'clock. The children will have their own parade with pets following that. You may like that. Things can get comical during it." She went on to explain the booths would dismantle around noon. "Food trucks will be around all afternoon. Of course, the shops will be open."

"I hate to see it all end," Holly said. "It's been so much fun."

Mac reminded her that the real fun began with the fireworks and dancing all night long.

Once desserts were eaten, Melissa pulled Brenda aside. "I still want to interview you, Brenda. Will you have a few minutes tomorrow morning?"

Brenda and Melissa agreed nine in the morning would be a good time. Brenda promised a tour around nine-thirty to anyone interested. Several showed interest. "I'll give you the history of each room and the décor in them. Randolph had an avid awareness of artifacts, especially those that pertained to this Queen Anne and Sweetfern Harbor." Conversations flowed about the subject until all except two guests decided to join the tour the next morning.

Glen walked behind Harry down the driveway. "Where's Colleen?"

"She's waiting for Melissa. They'll join me at Harbor Park." Harry had no guilt this time about walking without his dismal wife alongside him. A few minutes later, he stopped when he heard his name called. Colleen walked quickly toward them. "Where's Melissa?" Harry asked her.

"She said she'd meet us down there in a few minutes. She had something to do first."

By the time Melissa got to Harbor Park, she could see no sign of the Sullivans. She felt a presence next to her and turned to see Glen Adams beside her.

"Are you staying for the dance tonight?" Glen said.

"I'm not sure. I plan to enjoy the fireworks first and then decide." They chatted for a few more minutes until darkness covered the park. It was time for the big display. The mayor announced contributors to the fireworks and then gave the signal to begin. The lake suddenly burst into rockets and multicolored lights to the admiration of the onlookers. Melissa wondered where Colleen and Harry had gone. Between pauses, she looked for them.

"Have you seen the Sullivans?" Melissa asked Glen.

"I walked down here with them, but then they became distracted with things going on along the way. I don't know what happened to them."

Glen slightly bumped into Melissa as if someone jarred him. He apologized. Melissa noted that no one was so close to them as to have knocked into him. She smiled to herself and decided to put up with his awkward approach. A few minutes before the fireworks ended, Holly and Luke joined them. Chance Rogers carried a cardboard tray of cold drinks. He offered one to everyone in the group.

"What about you, Chance? It seems you ran out," Melissa said.

"I had one already. Isn't this great? I don't think I've seen a display like Sweetfern Harbor puts on." Approval spread across his face. The others agreed with him.

The crowd began to disperse in different directions. Glen spoke to Melissa. "I must apologize, Melissa. I doubt I'll last through the entire night dancing, but if you'd like one with me, I'll be happy to indulge."

Chance looked at his fellow fireman. He had never known a time when Glen Adams didn't want to party when he had the chance.

"I'll be fine," Melissa said. Seeing Glen stifle a yawn, she said, "It looks like the day is catching up with you." She looked around her. "I'm sure I'll find someone to dance with." Glen's heart missed a beat when he saw the twinkle in her eye. Still, he kept to his decision to leave the group. Inwardly, Melissa wondered if Glen bumping into her earlier was accidental after all and not a lame attempt at flirting.

"I keep imagining that big comfortable bed in my room at the bed and breakfast." Glen excused himself again and left the group. He didn't notice Chance's stare that followed him.

Chance was the first to offer Melissa a dance. She took him up on it and was surprised at his agility and talent. One after another exchanged dancing partners until Chance put his hand up. It had been quite a while since Glen had left the group.

"I'm afraid I'm ready to follow Glen to the B&B. It's been most enjoyable," Chance said. "We have a long drive home tomorrow. I look forward to a good night's sleep." He smiled when Holly reminded him that most of the night had slipped away.

When Chance walked up the drive to the Sheffield Bed and Breakfast, he paused to take it all in. Soft lights shone through the windows from common areas of the inn. Walkway lights outlined the pathways that wound around both sides of the structure. He listened to the waves lapping against the beach and the far end of the seawall. He felt he could live the rest of his life hanging on to the calmness of this scene before him.

There was no light from under the door of Glen's room.

Chance smiled to himself and shook his head. He couldn't help but wonder why his partner left a party so early.

CHAPTER SIX

Detective Mac Rivers took his wife's hand. "I must say, Brenda, this has been an event with very few arrests. They were all due to inebriated partygoers who pushed their limits."

"It has been a wonderful weekend, Mac."

Bryce and Jenny stood beside them. "We're leaving now. We want to pick Nicholas up and go home," Jenny said. "He will be in the parade tomorrow with his puppy, Bear. I don't know how that will work out." Jenny told her father and Brenda that both child and puppy would be secured in a stroller.

"It is the most decorated of all," Bryce said. No one asked him how he knew that, but the pride that spilled over among all of them caused it to be insignificant.

"We'll be watching," Brenda said.

The couple left. Brenda realized this was the first time she'd had a chance to ask Mac about any record of the missing Marcy Scott.

"We have found nothing about her. It seems she is not in

any database outside this area, either. I wonder if the name is incorrect."

"That is strange, for sure," Brenda said. "Melissa said that Colleen found the photo in her yearbook, and later online with an updated picture. It mentioned in her information that a Marcy Scott had gone missing."

"That's what makes it all so mysterious. I believe that someone somewhere along the line realized there was no Marcy Scott missing. Perhaps they found the real name, but there is nothing on the wire about that." Mac brushed his hand back through his hair. "I don't understand it, unless Colleen has her information wrong."

"The last name Scott isn't uncommon," Brenda said. "Maybe the sister isn't the woman who is missing." Brenda shook her head as if to clear her mind. "There is something not right about any of it."

Mac pointed in the direction of the makeshift dance floor. "The final three couples seem to finally have given up. Let's go home, Brenda."

Officer Thompson told Mac he would check in at the precinct for any updates. "Officer Sims is there, but she's ready to end her shift."

Mac thanked him for his work. "Things seem to have gone quite well." Officer Thompson agreed with his boss.

Brenda followed Mac in her car. Most of the lights in the guest rooms in the bed and breakfast had been extinguished. They went into their cottage. Sleep came easily to both of them.

Brenda and Mac slept an extra hour the next morning before finally agreeing it was time to get up. Chef Pierre had posted that breakfast would be extended an hour longer in case late-night partiers decided to sleep in. All had done so except for Chance Rogers and Melissa Harris. They were the only two guests in the dining room. Brenda greeted them and then went into the kitchen. Chef Pierre told her that Phyllis was in her old apartment waiting to have coffee with her. He handed Brenda a tray with a fresh pot of coffee and two coffee cups.

"Hope has already delivered fresh cinnamon rolls and bagels." He placed samples on the tray.

"She must not have gone to bed at all," Brenda said. "I noticed that she and David didn't leave the dance floor until late."

"I asked Hope how she had managed so early. She told me she and David went to Sweet Treats and prepared everything after the dance. According to her, it was simply a matter of slipping them into the ovens this morning."

"When does she plan to sleep?"

"She's probably in bed right now," Pierre said. "She arranged for two employees to take over the shop today."

Brenda joined Phyllis. Phyllis chatted first about the previous day's events. Then she began to discuss tasks for the day. "Do you know when guests will be checking out, Brenda?"

"Allie told me two on the third floor will check out this morning. I think everyone else will be gone by mid to late afternoon." She sipped her coffee. "Don't worry about getting to the rooms too soon, Phyllis. We scheduled no new guests until three days from now. Let's go join the ones who are up for a hot breakfast."

Melissa reminded Brenda of the interview. "I haven't forgotten that," Brenda said. "I'm looking forward to it."

By the time they finished eating, all guests had come in except Colleen and Harry. Brenda had hoped to find a way to bring up the subject of siblings Colleen may have. She planned to word it in a way that others would be asked the same question. For now, she and Mac kept their promise not to reveal what Melissa had told them.

A few of the guests drank juice and coffee before excusing themselves. "We decided to go down for the pancake breakfast," Luke said. "I hope you don't mind."

Brenda waved her hand. "Go ahead and enjoy it. Chef Pierre is cooking as everyone comes in rather than the full breakfast all at once."

Holly and Luke left. Soon, Phyllis excused herself. "I'm going to get started in the Gathering Room and straighten that up first."

Brenda sat there for another half hour in hopes that Colleen and Harry would arrive soon. Finally, she gave up, thinking she must have missed them when she was having coffee with Phyllis.

"Thanks, Pierre. Our guests have thoroughly enjoyed the food you've served throughout the weekend. I appreciate how accommodating you are during event weekends."

Pierre smiled and accepted the compliments. He sat down with Brenda. "Are you waiting for someone to come in? I can be on standby while I get my aides busy clearing the tables now."

Brenda shook her head no. "I hoped to talk to the Sullivans, but I think they must have opted for the pancake breakfast. Go ahead and do whatever you need to do. I don't think anyone else will come in to eat this late."

Brenda joined Melissa for the interview. "I'll make it short, Brenda, since I'll take notes during the tour." Brenda was impressed with the intelligent questions Melissa asked. Everything she wanted to know was right on point with the topic. They left Brenda's office to join the ones who waited to tour. Brenda felt she was in her element when it came to this part of her obligations as hostess. She was pleased with the questions and curiosity of her guests.

"Are there any hidden passages here?" one guest asked.

Brenda stopped midway down the hall on the second

floor. She pointed to a section of the wall. "There is a closed off narrow passageway behind this wall. We discovered it one Halloween by accident. It leads to the back stairway. Barely one person at a time can nudge through it. We keep it closed off for safety reasons."

That seemed to satisfy everyone, though a few had hoped to see it for themselves. By the time they returned to the front foyer, the guests held a new appreciation of the history of the Sheffield Bed and Breakfast. They were most impressed with the focus Randolph Sheffield had in restoring it.

Brenda decided to return to the cottage for a cup of hot tea. She had fifteen minutes to make it downtown in time to see her and Mac's two-year-old grandson parade down the street with his puppy, Bear. She rinsed her cup quickly and brushed her hair again. As she got into her car, her cell phone rang.

"Brenda, where are you?" Mac said.

"I'm just leaving for the kiddie parade. I'll see you down there."

"We have a murdered victim in Harbor Park. The body was found behind the last pavilion. I had officers directing clean-up crews when the body was discovered."

"Who is it?"

"It's early yet. I'm on my way down there now. At this point, I have no idea who it is. Meet me down there."

Brenda knew Jenny would be disappointed if they didn't show up to see Nicholas in his first parade. On the other hand, Jenny had grown up with a dad who was often called out for emergencies such as this. Even so, Brenda knew she would feel bad about it. Brenda called Jenny, who answered right away.

"We're about ready to line up, Brenda." Brenda told her what was going on. She heard an audible sigh. "I understand.

There's nothing you can do about it. I'll take lots of pictures and you can see us later."

Jenny's mother had passed away when Jenny was young. She grew up under the care of her detective father and a faithful nanny who stayed with them until Jenny was old enough to be home alone. Even then, Faith often stayed at their house in case Mac had an emergency call. Mac finally arranged for her to move permanently into a small apartment he renovated just for her. She still lived there now that Jenny and Bryce had a small child. Jenny, Bryce, and Nicholas lived in the same house Jenny grew up in.

Thankful for Jenny's understanding but still feeling guilty, Brenda drove to Harbor Park.

When she reached Mac, the body had been covered and was ready to be put onto the coroner's gurney. Mac told Brenda the body had been identified as Colleen Scott Sullivan. Brenda's hand flew to her mouth.

"How long has she been here?"

"We think she was killed sometime last night. The coroner will have more information soon for us." Brenda asked the manner of death. "The marks on her neck indicate that possibly something like a belt was used to strangle her, but that isn't definite at this point."

"Where is Harry? Does he know she's dead?"

Mac shook his head. "We're in the process of locating him. He may still be at the bed and breakfast."

"I don't think so. I waited for him and Colleen for quite a while past breakfast serving. Neither of them came into the dining room. Of course, I see why Colleen didn't." Brenda looked at the covered body. "I'd like to see her before they take her."

Mac indicated to the coroner to allow Brenda to look at the body. Brenda started with the top of Colleen's dark hair. Her eyes scanned down the face until they landed on the woman's neck. Brenda bent to take a closer look. She thought it could have been a belt. There were no rough marks as if a cord or rope had been used. Then she saw a slight indentation on the right side of her neck.

"Turn her onto her left side slightly, please," Brenda said.

She pointed out to Mac the marking that she thought was from the edge of a belt buckle. The coroner told her he had noticed that as well.

"We'll be thorough, Brenda. By the time I'm finished, we'll know what caused the murder." Brenda had no reason to doubt the coroner's word. She pulled the cover back over Colleen's body, sad that the troubled woman had met such a tragic end.

"I wonder if this could have anything to do with her missing sister, Mac. What do you think?"

"I don't know, but it's very possible. It could be someone out to get her and her sister, too."

Brenda knew that anyone close in kin to Colleen would have to be notified. The first to meet that criteria would be Harry Sullivan. Brenda thought about Colleen's parents—if they were still alive, that is. How would they react knowing they had lost two daughters?

Allie Williams heard footsteps on the staircase. She looked up to see Harry Sullivan descending. He looked as if he'd had a long night of revelry. "You missed breakfast, Harry, but I'm sure Chef Pierre can find something for you to eat."

"Thanks, I'll wait until lunch." His crooked smile was one of guilt for sleeping so late. "Have you seen Colleen? I hope she hasn't given up on me."

"She may be downtown. She wasn't here for breakfast."

"I'll just grab some coffee and go find her."

While he was speaking with Chef Pierre, Allie answered the call from Brenda.

CHAPTER SEVEN

As soon as Allie heard the news of Colleen's death, she asked Brenda who should tell Harry.

"He was looking for her a few minutes ago. He mentioned that he had a little too much to drink last night and wasn't sure if she even came in or not."

"I'll come home and tell him, Allie. Please ask him to wait until I get there if he decides to go look for her."

When the call ended, Glen Adams walked in the front door. Allie looked at him and frowned. She was sure he wore the same clothes he had on the afternoon before. She'd had a short conversation with him then and he had told her he looked forward to the rest of the celebrations.

"It looks like you had a long night of celebrations, Glen," Harry said. He came from the Gathering Room with a cup of coffee in his hand. "I'd say you overdid it. Are you just now getting in?"

Glen produced a sheepish smile. "I came in last night before most did. I was bushed and went right to bed. I've been down on the beach still trying to wake up." Harry commented that he looked as if he had slept on the beach. Glen ignored the remark.

Either Harry hadn't noticed or chose to ignore it, but no one mentioned the fact that the fireman wore the same clothing as the day before. Melissa came from the hall that led to the kitchen. She cupped a mug of hot chocolate in her hands and looked at Glen. Her eyes met Allie's. She validated by her expression that they agreed he hadn't changed clothes. Allie wondered if he had slept in them or if he really ever went to bed.

Allie caught Harry before he went out the door. "Brenda asked me to have you wait here for her, Harry. She'll be here in a few minutes."

"I hope she's seen Colleen. It will save me time searching for her. She's not answering her phone." Harry sat in the antique loveseat that was set against the wall. Allie smiled at him. He obviously had no idea his wife was dead. Then he stood up again.

"I think I'll take a walk outside. I'll stick close by, Allie, until Brenda gets here."

"I'll let her know where you are."

Glen weaved a little to gain his balance and then slowly walked up the stairs. Once he was out of earshot, Allie said to Melissa, "Glen looks like he's had quite a night of it."

Melissa shook her head. "It's weird. Glen left us early last night. He said he was coming back here to go to bed. I thought he faked his yawn when he was leaving us. I wonder where he spent the night."

"I have no idea. I do know he is wearing the same clothes he had on yesterday when I saw him. I guess he could have changed out of them before the festivities last night and just put them back on this morning."

Melissa chuckled. "He didn't change clothes. He's

wearing exactly what he wore throughout the day and evening."

Chance Rogers ambled down the passageway from the kitchen area. The fact that he was so relaxed added to his physical appeal. He carried a cup of coffee with him. "I've been visiting with the chef. I thought it was time to let him know how much I'm enjoying the food that comes from his kitchen. I've never tasted anything like it."

Melissa didn't realize she was staring at Chance until his eyes rested on her long enough to cause an inward squirm. She faced Allie. "I think I'll go find Colleen. We have a lot in common when it comes to shopping."

Chance told them he was going to his room and then to the beach. When Melissa was sure he couldn't hear her, she commented to Allie about how good-looking a "man of his age" was. He hid his smile when he turned at the landing to complete the steps.

Brenda rushed in. "Did you keep Harry around?"

"He's taking a walk around the grounds. He left his cell phone number. I'll call him to let him know you're here."

"Never mind. I'll find him," Brenda said. Back outside, Brenda's eyes gazed over the gardens and side yard. She spotted Harry Sullivan near the seawall. When he saw her, he started walking in her direction.

"Let's find a bench and sit down," Brenda said. They settled on the padded stone bench where peonies were in full bloom around them. "I have some news to give you, Harry. It isn't good."

Harry focused on Brenda. "I had hoped you'd found my wife. I haven't been able to locate her since I got up."

"She has been found. Harry, I'm so sorry, but I'm afraid she is dead."

Harry shot up from the bench. His face paled. He paced

a few steps and turned back to Brenda. "Wait. Are you sure it isn't someone else? Where is she?"

"She was discovered in Harbor Park behind one of the pavilions by a clean-up crew. She has been identified."

"I-I don't understand. How did she die?"

Brenda took a deep breath. "She was apparently strangled to death. We'll know more when the coroner is ready to divulge manner of death."

Harry sat back down. He dipped his head in his hands. His elbows rested on his knees. No tears managed to flow at this point. Brenda knew there weren't always immediate tears when news like this was received. He had asked the questions she hoped he would. For now, he seemed genuinely shocked at the news. "I'd like for you to come down to the precinct for some questioning after you make a positive identification for us."

Harry faced her. "Are you looking at me as the one who killed her?"

"No one is a suspect yet, Harry. We start with those closest to a victim in order to find who did such a thing. You can tell us when you saw her last and if there is any reason you can think of that could cause someone to commit murder."

Harry relaxed somewhat. "I'll do all I can to get to the bottom of this. I just can't believe this." He followed Brenda to the coroner's office to verify that the victim was his wife. Then he entered the police station with Brenda. Mac stood and shook Harry's hand. He offered sincere condolences.

"We will get to the bottom of this, Harry." Mac saw that Harry appeared to be in a stupor. The shock remained set in him. "When did you see Colleen last?"

"Well…I wanted to go to the parade, but she wasn't interested. She said she wanted to walk along the shoreline and breathe in the ocean air. She knew most people would be downtown and she wanted peace and quiet. At least, those were her words. I went with her."

"How long were you down there?" Mac said.

"I gave her the time she needed while I sat on a rock and watched the boats. I'd say we spent over an hour there. I finally asked her if she was ready to go back to the festivities. I thought she needed some fun in her life for a change. She said she wasn't interested in having fun."

"Why did the two of you come here if not to enjoy the weekend?" Mac leaned forward. "And what was she upset about? Everyone noticed she clearly wasn't happy."

For the first time, Harry settled more comfortably in the chair. "She was sure that her missing sister was in this area. Her only intention was to find her. She'd built up a fan base that included many who had missing loved ones. Someone on that site told her that her sister, Marcy Scott, had been spotted in this region. Colleen decided to begin searching right here."

"Did she have any idea about how her sister went missing?" Brenda said.

Harry shook his head as if exasperated. "To tell you the truth, my belief is that there was no sister to begin with. I met Colleen's parents on occasion in their home before we married. I never saw any photos of a sister around. They displayed various poses of Colleen as she grew up. Several on the wall were of her and her parents taken over the years." He paused. "I think a couple of photos may have been her grandparents."

"Did you ask her point-blank if she really had a sister at all?" Brenda waited and watched.

"Many times. Every time she got off on the subject, I asked for details. She said she was the sister that her parents kept hidden from her. She always thought they had something to do with her disappearance. Colleen firmly believed her parents gave her sister away. She had no idea the woman existed until about five years ago. Then, two years ago, she saw an article about someone named Marcy Scott who had vanished. It set her on a wild tailspin. After that, she became consumed with finding this woman she was convinced was her sister."

Brenda and Mac asked further questions regarding the vanished sister. Harry answered with facts they had already heard about from Melissa Harris.

Mac told him to think about anyone who was friends with Colleen, as well as any enemies she may have had. "We'll need her parents' names and phone number. We'll talk more with you later today."

Harry stood up and shook Mac's hand again after providing the information. "I'm into reading all sub-genres of mysteries. I've taken it on myself to try to solve cold cases, too." His mouth curved slightly. "Of course, I don't mean I outwardly solve them, but I do so as a hobby of mine. I find cold cases fascinating." He turned around at the door. "Let me know if I can get in on this case. I may find some answers for you."

Brenda and Mac looked at each other. "We'll use you as a possible witness to this crime, Harry," Mac said. "She was married to you. We need personal information to build the case. I'm sure you are anxious to find out who killed her, but you need to allow us to do our job."

After Harry Sullivan left, Brenda said, "That was bizarre. He suddenly looked at this as something totally removed from him."

"Something about him is certainly strange, Brenda. Perhaps it is his way of coping, if he can put himself at a distance."

"Maybe." Brenda didn't agree with Mac's comment at all. "I think he should be kept under observation. We need to speak to him again very soon. I don't want to give him time to come up with his own opinions."

Mac's eyebrows rose. He repositioned a folder on his desk. "I'm going to look to see if Harry Sullivan has any priors. Feel free to talk with him again. We do need a list of her friends as well as possible enemies or people who held a grudge for whatever reason. And Harry should notify her parents as soon as possible."

Allie greeted Brenda when she returned to the B&B. Brenda was deep in thought as she recalled the times that she noticed Harry and Colleen interacting. They seemed compatible enough when she paid attention to them.

"Word has spread around here, Brenda, about Colleen's death. Everyone has their own take on what happened."

Brenda became more alert. "Did you see Harry come back?" Allie shook her head no. "I'll find him later," Brenda said.

"I thought you already talked with him."

"We did, but I have more questions to ask him." Brenda stopped talking. She listened to the buzzing conversations that came from the Gathering Room. Melissa Harris apparently felt free to open up more about Colleen's reasons for being in Sweetfern Harbor. There was no controlling gossip that inevitably would find its way around town. Melissa emerged from the Gathering Room.

"Did Allie tell you how one of the firemen looked earlier?" Melissa said. "He was quite a sight."

Brenda looked at Allie, who said, "It's just that we were both surprised to see that he was wearing the very same clothes he had on all day yesterday. I'm sorry, Brenda, I know I'm not supposed to pass judgment on our guests, but it was hard to miss."

"Especially after he told the rest of us that he was coming straight back here to turn in early. That's what added to it all.

I think he must have crashed on the beach from the way he looked," Melissa said. "He left the celebrations after the fireworks ended. He told me earlier how much he liked to dance, and yet he left before he danced once. He even said he'd ask me to dance, but then he never did. It was very strange."

"Who are you talking about?"

"Glen Adams, the younger fireman," Allie said.

CHAPTER EIGHT

Brenda went to the cottage. She wanted to talk with Mac on her cell with no interruptions. She told him about the remarks Melissa and Allie made about Glen Adams. Mac suggested she talk with him next.

"If you draw any conclusions that warrant a more thorough interview, bring him down here."

"Did you find Colleen's parents?"

"We notified them. It seems Harry hadn't gotten around to letting them know. They are on their way up here now."

Brenda found Glen Adams. He was clean-shaven. His clothing was pressed, and he looked more alert than Brenda expected. She asked if she could speak with him for a few minutes. He agreed with no hesitation. He also agreed to be taped.

Brenda offered him something to drink. He declined. "How well did you know the Sullivans before coming here?"

Glen jerked back and then asked why she thought he knew them before this weekend.

"I'm sure you've heard the news by now about Colleen."

"I've been upstairs in my room. What's going on?"

"She was found early this morning strangled to death." Brenda watched his reaction closely. He didn't flinch.

"I had not heard that. I'm sure Harry is devastated." Brenda began to wonder why he didn't ask questions about the victim's demise, and then he asked, "Where was she found?"

"Her body was discovered in Harbor Park. She was killed sometime during the night or possibly earlier. We're waiting for the coroner's report."

Glen shook his head. "That's too bad. She seemed like a very nice person."

"Where did you spend the night?"

"I admit I was a bum on the beach. I intended to take a walk in the sand before going to bed. Instead, I sat down and listened to the ocean. Before I knew it, I'd fallen asleep. I still have a sore neck from the position I was in."

"Can anyone verify that you spent the night down there?"

"I saw a few people when I first got there. I didn't know any of them." He gave a small grin. "I suppose I have no witnesses."

Brenda made a mental note to get a warrant to search his room. She wanted to affirm that there was sand in his clothing. She suddenly made a quick decision.

"Since it seems you can't produce witnesses, do you mind if I look at the clothing you were wearing last night?"

"Not at all. I'll get them for you. You won't enjoy handling them. They're gross from twenty-four hours of wear." Brenda followed him upstairs to his room. He bagged the clothing in a trash bag from the wastebasket and handed it to her.

"Thank you," Brenda said. "I'll get these back to you unless you want them laundered."

"I'll be leaving later today. I'll take them along and wash them at home."

Brenda examined the clothing in her office. She spread the pale tan afghan on the floor that she retrieved from the Gathering Room. Then, piece by piece, she shook the clothing. Very little sand fell. Most of what did came from the bottom part of the leg sections. She snapped photos and put the clothing back into the bag.

Brenda found Glen on the side lawn. "If you don't mind, I'd like to take the clothing down to the precinct for testing. I'll have them back to you before you leave."

At first, she thought he was going to refuse. "I suppose I should ask what this is all about. Am I a suspect in Colleen's murder?"

"We are scrutinizing everyone who had any contact with her at all. That means every guest here." Brenda didn't elaborate on the fact that so far, only his clothing was up for examination.

"Go ahead and take them. I know from my line of business that you'll get a search warrant if I don't cooperate. I have nothing to hide."

Mac called Brenda to tell her he was going to make a quick stop at the bed and breakfast. He wanted to ask Harry more questions. Brenda told him about the story that Glen Adams related to her, and about the clothing he gave permission to be tested. "I'm at the back gate now," Mac said. "Meet me out here."

Brenda carried the bag with her. Mac took it and told her he would take it to the lab right away. "I'll be back as soon as I drop it off."

"While you're doing that, I'm going down to Jonathan's shop on the beach."

When Brenda arrived at the boat rental shop, she was told that Jonathan was downtown taking his break. Brenda smiled. Jon always took his breaks at the Morning Sun Coffee Shop. It was his daily chance to be near Molly Lindsay.

"Did you work late last evening?" she asked the employee, Tim.

"I was here until around eight," Tim said. "We weren't doing much business at that hour. Jon told me to close up and go on down for the celebrations. I took him up on it."

"Did you see many people on the waterfront before you left?"

"A few hung around." Brenda gave him the description of Glen Adams. "I don't recall anyone like that. There was a couple here and a family with several kids. I'm sure they were the only ones in this area. Like I said, I left around eight. He could have come down after that."

Brenda decided to join Mac when he spoke with Harry again. She thought about Glen Adams. The more she searched for motives, the less she came up with. Brenda arrived at the front door of the B&B just as Mac pulled into the back driveway. They met near the kitchen.

"What did Jon have to say?" Mac said.

Brenda told him about her talk with Tim. "I have suspicions about Glen, but I haven't come up with any motive for him to kill Colleen." Mac commented they may have known one another before arriving this weekend. "That's the one possibility," Brenda said, "but he denied knowing either of the Sullivans until they checked in here."

Harry Sullivan spotted Brenda and the detective from the front foyer. He waved and smiled at them before reaching them. "Is there anything I can do to solve this mystery?"

Mac gritted his teeth. "We are doing everything we can at this point. Do you have a list of Colleen's friends and possible enemies?"

"Sure," Harry said. He pulled a folded sheet of paper from his shirt pocket. "I've listed friends of hers. She didn't have many because in the last few years she became a recluse, more or less. Colleen lost interest in socializing once she focused entirely on finding her sister."

Brenda was certain she caught him rolling his eyes. "You don't seem to have taken her search seriously. Did you support her?"

"I did my best. However, we began to lose touch with one another the more she obsessed about it. I told her to involve the police, but she refused because of one precinct that brushed her off."

Brenda had heard the story from Melissa. "Did you know any of our guests before you and Colleen arrived here?"

"I didn't know any of them. I was glad to see Colleen latch onto Melissa Harris. Melissa is upbeat, and I felt it would be good for Colleen to have a diversion. Instead, she confided in Melissa about the matter. Melissa encouraged my wife to go to the police, too. Again, she refused, as I expected."

"I'd like to hear a little more about your own background," Mac said. "What did you do before you began driving a concrete truck?"

"I tried college for two and a half years, then gave that up. I found it hard to study. Besides, I wanted to get on with my life. I started working with a landscape company before landing my present job with a construction company. I'm in my eighth year there."

"You said when you last saw Colleen, you were both on the beach," Brenda said. "What did you do after that?"

"I still wanted to go to the fireworks. I was sure she had recouped enough to join me. She told me she was going to stay at the waterfront a while longer. I gave up on her and headed for the park. She suddenly changed her mind and came with me. She agreed to watch from a distance. She shunned crowds."

"Did you see anyone there that you knew?"

"I saw plenty of people down there, Brenda, but if you are asking if I was with any of your guests, I didn't see any of them. Colleen left me to look for Melissa, I believe. That's the last time I saw her. There were some guys around my age who had been drinking. I overheard one of them say they were going to end the night at the Octopus Tavern. I asked them if they minded if I joined them. They were happy to have me along. I was there longer than I should have stayed before finding my way back here. I was sound asleep almost instantly."

"I'd like the names of the people you drank with," Mac said.

"I remember one name. If I heard any others, I was too drunk to recall them. The one I recall was named Jack someone." He produced a sheepish grin. "I don't have any idea who else I spent those hours with."

Brenda pressed him for memories of when or if Colleen had returned to their room. Harry told her he had no idea if she came to bed or not. "I wasn't in the best condition to be aware of anything. I'm sure she wasn't in bed when I got in, and she wasn't there when I woke up. I suppose she didn't come back at all, since you said she was killed sometime during the night."

Mac dismissed him. He looked at Brenda. "He doesn't seem all that wrought up about her death."

"I agree. He's handling it all in a very noncommittal manner."

Mac told her he was going back to the precinct but not before begging Chef Pierre for a bite to eat. Phyllis was dusting the frames of paintings in the hallway. She asked Brenda if she should tidy up the Sullivans' room yet.

"Leave it for now. I think Mac is getting a search warrant for that room. If you haven't cleaned the room Glen Adams is in, leave that one, too."

"I hadn't planned to clean that one until after he left. He told me that he and Chance will be checking out late this afternoon."

Brenda decided to go up the back stairs to the second floor. She had no concrete plan why but hoped to pick up something unusual. When she turned at the landing, she was surprised to meet Glen Adams. Guests rarely used the back staircase. He had an overnight bag in his hand. "Are you checking out now?"

"I'm putting a few things into the car, but we won't check out until late afternoon. I thought I'd get a head start on loading up."

"Michael will be glad to help you when you're ready."

"I can handle it."

Brenda hesitated. "I think Mac wants to look at everyone's room before they check out. He's getting warrants now." The steely eyes that met Brenda's were totally unexpected. "It is part of the routine. We are looking at everyone here who came to know Colleen."

Glen didn't speak. Then his shoulders slumped slightly. "I get it. Do you want me to leave this bag in my room then?"

"No, you can go ahead and put it in your car. He will have search warrants for vehicles."

Glen hesitated and then attempted an understanding smile. He stood aside to allow Brenda to continue up the stairs. Her first intent was to go into her old apartment, the one she had occupied before marrying Mac. The wide window provided a full view of the side lawn and back parking lot. This was the area used for employees, though sometimes guests parked there if they came up to the inn from the back way. She watched Glen Adams open the SUV and sling his overnight case inside. He then went to the side door behind the passenger seat. He appeared to be rummaging for something. She breathed a sigh of relief when he closed the door empty-handed.

CHAPTER NINE

The last of the celebrations ended downtown. The Sheffield Bed and Breakfast guests who saw festivities to the end walked back to the inn for lunch. Mac remained in his office listening to the latest reports concerning the murdered victim. Brenda joined the guests for lunch. It was a more somber group than usual. Melissa didn't hold back.

"Have they found out who killed Colleen?" she said. She apologized to Harry for being so blunt. "I shouldn't ask. I know this must be very difficult for you, Harry."

"It's all right," he said. "I want to know as much as possible about it." He turned to Brenda. "Is there anything new on the case?"

"Interviews are being conducted, as most of you already know. Mac will meet with those of you he hasn't talked with yet. If you can think of anyone who would want to cause Colleen harm in any way, please let us know."

"Have they completed canvassing the area where she was found?" Chance said.

"Officers are still down there. I'm sure specific evidence will be showing up soon." They discussed the matter for a few minutes longer. No one came up with a possible murderer.

"It could have been random," Holly said. "Maybe she was just in the wrong place at the wrong time. The crowds were large and noisy, too."

Brenda didn't have to address her remarks since the rest of them chimed in with their comments. She had thought it could have been random, but so far, the only conclusion to her attack was someone she knew had killed her. Her money, which consisted of three folded twenties, was still in her pocket. The card to get back into the B&B and her room were also there. It hadn't been a robbery gone bad. There were no physical marks on her other than the deep marks around her neck. Brenda glanced at her phone when it vibrated. She excused herself to take the call from Mac.

"We think we've found the murder weapon, Brenda. One of the officers directed the others to spread out further for anything that looked like an object to cause such a death. One found a belt under branches from a low bush. It has a unique belt buckle." He described the brass buckle.

"I'll be right down," Brenda said.

"You can meet Colleen's parents then. They just arrived."

Brenda went back into the dining room and told her guests to enjoy the rest of the meal. She excused herself and left for the precinct. She wanted to get a good look at the brass buckle. Something in the back of her mind nagged at her.

"This is Ruth and Daniel Scott, Brenda," Mac said when she entered his office.

Brenda acknowledged the introduction and expressed her sympathies. Ruth Scott found it difficult to hold back tears that threatened to spill. Daniel Scott remained stoic as if to control his own emotions.

"I've given them as many details as we know so far," Mac said. He didn't mention the belt and signature belt buckle.

Brenda and Mac allowed the Scotts to express their frustration on what had happened to their daughter. "She chose to become a stranger to us these last few years," Ruth said. "She got it into her head that we'd kept a sister from her. Nothing we said or did could convince her that she had always been an only child." Ruth sniffed twice before reaching for a tissue. "Colleen was adamant about seeing a photo of someone who looked like her. She always wished for a sister, but she was our only child. The photo was of someone older than she was but with the same last name." Ruth wrung her hands. "I hope that whole thing wasn't the cause of such a terrible death for her."

Daniel wiped his eyes with the back of his hand. He composed himself and spoke. "Colleen was a good child. Even when she insisted that we had somehow gotten rid of the sister she was sure she had, there were times I still saw the old Colleen again. It never lasted."

Brenda exchanged a quick glance with Mac. They didn't doubt the truth of what the Scotts told them. "I ask this simply to clarify the matter," Brenda said. "You are telling us that whoever this Marcy Scott is, she isn't your daughter?"

"No, she is not," Ruth said. "Did Colleen convince you she was her sister, too?"

"She didn't tell us anything. However, she befriended one of our guests and told her about it," Mac said. He leaned in. "How well do you know Harry Sullivan?"

The Scotts widened their eyes simultaneously. "Colleen introduced him to us after they had been dating for several months," Daniel said. "I never understood why she didn't want a big wedding. We didn't know him at all, but as time went by, they came by on occasion. I suppose we got to know him as well as expected."

"You don't believe Harry had anything to do with this, do you?" Ruth said.

"We haven't drawn any conclusions at all," Mac said. "We're trying to get to know everyone who knew Colleen. Harry provided the names of three friends of hers and stated she didn't have any more."

Ruth sat still. "She had many friends before she met Harry and married him. I can't blame him for her losing friends, though. Once her obsession began over this non-existent sister, I'm sure few people wanted to be around her."

When asked if their daughter had enemies, her parents shook their heads. "I'm not saying that everyone she met liked her, but as for the term *enemies*, I think if someone didn't like her, she just withdrew from that person," Daniel said. His wife agreed.

Brenda noted the fatigue that set in on Ruth and Daniel. "I have one last question to ask. I'm sure you'd like to get settled in at the hotel and get some rest." Ruth nodded. Daniel told her to go ahead and ask. "Do you know a fireman by the name of Glen Adams?"

Their foreheads wrinkled. After a few seconds, both stated they did remember that he was in the papers for rescuing two children from a housefire. "We didn't know him personally. He got an award of some kind for his bravery."

Daniel chimed in. "The family of the children also gave him a special belt buckle that had an inscription on it. Do you remember what it was, Ruth?" She didn't recall the presentation at all. When she asked how Glen Adams was related to their daughter's murder, Brenda told her they were unable to give them any information.

After they left, Brenda asked to see the belt. Mac took

her to the evidence room. The brass buckle gleamed. She pulled gloves on and took the belt from the evidence bag. "I've seen this before. Let me think." Brenda snapped her fingers. "I remember it now. Glen Adams and Chance Rogers checked in a day early. I'm sure this is the buckle that caught my eye. Glen Adams wore it. I'm sure of it." When she saw his name on it, her recall was affirmed.

Mac sent one of his officers to the bed and breakfast to bring the firefighter in for questioning.

In the meantime, Ruth Scott called Mac. "We forgot to mention that Harry Sullivan asked us a couple of years ago about Colleen. He asked about the sister she learned she had. We assured him she had no sister at all. He thanked us and hung up. We think he stood by her, though he knew the truth."

Mac passed the latest information on to Brenda. "We have two suspects. The belt belongs to Glen Adams. The husband knew long ago that Colleen had no missing sister."

"Perhaps they are both involved in her murder," Brenda said, "but what reason would Glen have to murder her?"

"That's what we must find out."

Glen Adams acted astounded that he was being suspected of murder. Chance followed the police car to the station. He waited in the reception area while his partner was being questioned. He fully expected Glen to ride back to the B&B with him. Instead, he learned that Glen had been charged with murder. Shock set in. Chance Rogers sat where he waited until Brenda came from the narrow hallway to the front entrance.

"Brenda, what's going on?"

"I'm not at liberty to give any details out. I can say that we may have evidence that points to Glen. If Colleen's DNA matches what we've found, I'm afraid Glen has become our prime suspect in her murder."

Chance rubbed his forehead. "He told me yesterday that he couldn't locate a belt a family gave him when he rescued their children from a fire. He was very upset about the matter. Have you found his belt?"

"We found something that could have been the murder weapon. I'm not at liberty to give any details of the investigation."

The firefighter looked at Brenda. "You have the wrong person. Someone has set him up. This was a preplanned murder that I feel is indicated by his belt being stolen before the murder. If that's what you found, he didn't use it to kill anyone."

Brenda hesitated. Glen had not reported any stolen property to her or to Mac. She asked Chance why Glen hadn't let them know he was missing something. "He thought he had just misplaced it. He finally laughed about it and said it would turn up soon. Where was it found exactly?"

"I didn't say we found his belt. I can't discuss this matter further with you."

"I've known Glen Adams since he was a rookie. It's not in his bones to kill anyone. His entire focus in life is saving others. I don't think he even knew Colleen Sullivan until he met her and Harry at your bed and breakfast." He shook his head. "He isn't your killer."

Brenda asked him to tell Mac what he told her. He did, and, at the end, Chance reiterated that they didn't have the right person. "I have no idea if his belt was the murder weapon, but if it was, someone left it there to make it look as if he is the murderer."

Mac felt his story was plausible. Glen hadn't wavered from his insistence they had the wrong man. On the other hand, many suspects often insisted they were innocent.

"If you keep him here, I will call his lawyer in for defense."

"He will be here overnight. I'll present the case to the judge and get his opinion. In the meantime, you are free to call an attorney if that is what Glen wants. It's probably a good idea that you do, in fact." Mac watched the expression on Chance's face. He was determined to stand up for his partner.

After he left, Brenda sat back down. "What do you think?"

"I think he could be right about Glen's innocence," Mac said, "but the fact remains that it was his belt that was found at the scene. It isn't time to tell anyone that. I'll try to hurry up the DNA results. The sooner we get that, the sooner we can determine it is the murder weapon."

Brenda recalled Glen's sense of humor. His lighthearted personality didn't come across as that of a murderer. His eyes expressed his feelings when he talked, so he was no psychopath. If he had been, likely no emotions of any kind would have been obvious. Mac questioned Brenda why no one reported anything missing from Sheffield's.

"According to Chance, Glen felt sure he had misplaced it. He told him it would show up when least expected. I suppose he was right about that."

An hour later, Chance Rogers called the precinct. "His lawyer will arrive in a half hour. In the meantime, he and I will post bond to release Glen."

Mac told him he would speak to a judge before the day was over to see if a bond was set. Later, the judge listened to the entire story. He decided a bond could be posted but that Glen had to stay in town. By eight that night, Glen Adams was back at the bed and breakfast with Chance. They offered to stick around the B&B rather than find another hotel. As Chance put it, "We want to see this through to the end when you get the right person."

Brenda felt fatigue setting in. She told Mac she was going

to check things out at the bed and breakfast and then go to their cottage. When she walked into the inn, she saw Glen and Harry down the hallway. They spoke briefly and ended the conversation with a chuckle between them. Brenda made a mental note of their behavior before heading home.

CHAPTER TEN

Brenda greeted her remaining guests the next morning. Chance and Glen sat together. Both were courteous toward Brenda. Harry walked through the buffet line, choosing scrambled eggs, bacon, and wheat toast. At the last minute, he swerved around and grabbed orange juice. He joined Brenda and the firefighters.

"I'm glad you got sprung, Glen. How does it feel being on the outside?"

Brenda pushed the surge of anger down. Glen didn't answer at first. "I should have never been arrested," he said. He faced Brenda. "I know it was your job to consider me as the culprit."

Brenda could barely swallow her last sip of coffee before excusing herself. She met Mac just as he went into the kitchen. She followed him. Mac knew when his wife was upset, though no words were spoken. He asked her what was wrong. Brenda repeated the conversation at the table.

"I need some fresh air, Mac. I think I'll go down to the ocean and recoup for a few minutes." As soon as she left, she called Mac. "I've changed my mind. If you need me, I'll be at the crime scene."

Two officers remained at the park. She asked if they had found anything new. They shook their heads no.

"We're still combing the area. The lab has gathered our discoveries so far."

Brenda asked for details. She was told several hairs had been found near the location of the body plus a handprint. Colleen had been lying on a sparse patch of ground where the grass was not abundant. The print was to the left of her body, as if the killer had steadied himself to stand up.

Back at the B&B, Mac ate his cereal and toast. He chatted briefly with Chef Pierre and left for work. He heard his name called when he had his hand on the doorknob of the back door.

"If you have a minute, Detective, I want to ask you something." Harry frowned as if something serious was on his mind. Mac thought perhaps the shock had worn off and he was finally beginning to realize the gravity of the death of his wife.

"I wonder if I can tag along with you today. I may be able to add information you'll need to solve Colleen's murder."

The detective fought to stay calm. "I don't have anything for you to do right now, Harry. I will call you if anything comes up."

Harry started to insist, but Mac was through the door before he had time to do so. When Mac arrived at his office, he was informed Colleen's parents were waiting for him in the front reception area. He told his clerk to give him ten minutes and he would speak to them in his office. Brenda came through the back door of the precinct.

"The officers out at the scene said they have sent a handprint to the lab." She explained where it was found.

"Officer Thompson called me on my way in. This may be the evidence to seal the deal." Mac flicked a pencil back and forth between his thumb and index finger. "I'm going to check on the belt results. Why don't you come with me?"

The lab technician groaned when she saw Mac and Brenda through the glass. It was always as such. Detective Mac Rivers had little patience when it came to them taking time to do their job. She told him they hoped to have results back later in the day. "We are being particularly careful so as not to make any mistakes. You don't want faulty evidence thrown out of court."

Brenda smiled at her. She knew her husband's impatience. "They are doing all they can, Mac. Let's go speak with the Scotts."

Ruth Scott stood up and expressed her thanks for the time the detective and Brenda were willing to give them. Daniel repeated her words.

"We have all the time it takes for you," Brenda said. "Do you have anything to add that you may have missed yesterday?"

"You asked if we knew Glen Adams. We talked about him last night, and Daniel recalled we had met him the night he received the award. I remembered it after he reminded me."

Daniel picked up the story. "What made it unusual that night was that Colleen and Harry were there. Of course, Colleen had chosen to sever ties with us by that time, so we didn't even get a chance to speak to them. I noticed Harry gave the fireman a hearty handshake as if he knew him personally. Colleen seemed to be offering her congratulations to him."

"Did they remain together the rest of the evening?" Brenda said.

"Right after that, Colleen and Harry left the building.

We both were convinced all three knew one another well. There was no reason to question it at the time. It seemed perfectly normal they would know people not in our circles." Daniel looked at his wife.

"When you asked if we knew Glen Adams, that scene at the awards ceremony didn't come to mind," Ruth said. "We simply got in line to congratulate him for his heroic actions. I don't think he said anything except thank you to us, as he did everyone else who filed through." She smiled. "I don't wish to take up your time, but I know you are in the middle of finding out who killed our daughter." She pulled a tissue from her purse. "This probably has no significance to the crime at all, but you did tell us to let you know of anything we remembered."

Mac thanked them. "Is there anything we can do for you now?"

"Just find out who took our daughter from us," Daniel said. He wiped his eyes with the back of his hand as he turned to go.

Brenda closed the office door behind them. "That's interesting. I think it was a good move not to tell them that the firefighter is one of our guests." Mac nodded.

Chance Rogers sat on the beach with his partner. Glen had once confided in him about his past. The younger fireman had been raised in a dysfunctional family. His father was an alcoholic. His mother eventually started taking drugs to cope. He and his brother scavenged for food in the back alley of a mom-and-pop grocery store. The owners felt sorry for them and gave them sandwiches to eat. They were elated when he handed them cold drinks.

By the time Glen was sixteen, his brother had been gone from home for two years and worked along the docks. It was a turning point for Glen Adams. The grocery owner took him under his wing and vowed to guide him in the right direction. One night, a fire destroyed the grocery. The man and wife succumbed to smoke inhalation.

When the shock and devastation of the situation hit Glen, he vowed to become a firefighter and do something with his life. He never looked back. Chance admired his determination.

"Who do you think killed Colleen Sullivan, Glen?"

"I don't know. I wish I did. I've thought about that evening a lot. Everyone we met here was with us at the fireworks except for Harry and Colleen. Harry told me they were down here on the beach because Colleen wanted to be away from the crowds."

"Did the detective or Brenda ask you if you knew the Sullivans before arriving here?"

"That was in the interrogation. I told them I didn't know them until recently."

"I've thought a lot about them," Chance said. "I felt I had seen them somewhere in the past. It was such a strong feeling that I really wracked my brain to remember. You did meet them once that I know of."

Glen jerked his head toward his partner. "What? When was that? I don't recall them at all."

"It was at your awards ceremony when you were singled out for your bravery when you rescued those two children."

"I definitely recall all of that. I never felt any of it merited all the uproar and notoriety anyway. I was doing what I was called to do in my job."

"Then you recall the long line of well-wishers."

Glen chuckled. "I have to say only those I already knew stuck out."

"The Sullivans weren't in the line. They caught up with you just before you got in position to receive your accolades.

I remember Harry giving you a big handshake. You had a brief conversation with him. Colleen stood by him, and she also congratulated you."

Glen thought hard for a few seconds. It hit him that Chance was right. "I do recall it now that you bring it up. That was them? I wish I had remembered them. I would have taken more time to visit with them while here." He took a small twig and made a design in the sand. "Poor Colleen. I wonder who wanted her dead."

"That is the mystery. I've drawn the conclusion one of the tourists in town did it. Maybe she resisted his advances and it came down to getting rid of her. I don't know. I heard she didn't have a purse with her."

"That was my idea at first," Glen said. "She was found in Harbor Park. Harry told me they were down here on the waterfront."

"I'm just glad I'm not the one to have to figure this out." Chance stood up and brushed the sand from his shorts. "I'm ready to start packing up. The boss back home reminded me last night we have a job to do there." Glen asked if he had told him about the arrest. "I had to. He didn't believe they had the right man, either, so don't worry. I suppose we should clear it with the detective about checking out. If they need us, they can find us easily enough."

After talking with the judge, Mac cleared the firemen to go on home. He reminded them to leave contact information with Allie or Brenda. Mac knew he had no reason to detain Glen Adams. Someone had stolen the belt and used it to frame Glen for the murder of Colleen Sullivan. He was sure of it.

Brenda wasn't so sure. True, he had plausible explanations for his actions, but she felt he could easily have had a part in it all. Back at the bed and breakfast, Brenda asked Allie if she had seen Harry. She gestured toward the Gathering Room. "He's in there looking out the window."

Brenda went in there and asked him to sit down. "When we asked you if you knew any of the guests before arriving here, you told us you knew none of them. We have reason to believe that you knew Glen Adams in the past."

"Not really. I knew who he was but had never met him. He got some kind of an award, as I recall. It was all over the news. I remember that."

Brenda decided it was time to quit beating around the bush. "We have witnesses who saw you at the awards ceremony. You spoke one on one with Glen, plus shook his hand. Colleen was next to you."

Harry's brow furrowed. "If I did that, it was Colleen's idea. She always gushed over anyone who was a celebrity."

"If you think hard enough, you will recall him." Brenda stood up and walked from the room.

Harry went to his room. He began packing his belongings, though aware he had been asked not to check out yet. Brenda and the detective didn't seem to realize he had a job that he still needed to do back home. He paused to really think about Colleen. Thoughts had sifted through his mind, but he hadn't concentrated on details surrounding her life yet. It hadn't taken long after their wedding vows were spoken for him to realize his wife was mentally unstable. He truly loved her. At first, it was easy to distract her from her wild notions.

He had even gone along with her concerns about the sister she never knew she had. Then, when Marcy Scott's photo spread across the newspapers and TV stations, he followed along with her drive to find the woman. He had given his all to his wife. Now, she would no longer be by his side.

Harry Sullivan huffed. He felt strongly that the cops weren't looking in the right places for her killer. If the detective would allow him on the case, he could direct them to where they should be going.

CHAPTER ELEVEN

"**A**re you making any progress, Brenda?" Mac said.

"Harry Sullivan seems to desperately want to be in on the case. I think his motive is more than the fact he likes to solve cold cases he hears about." Brenda rubbed her forehead. "I want to know more about Glen's missing belt. According to Chance, Glen cherished it. I think it holds great significance in his life. If it meant so much to him, why risk using it to kill someone and then toss it close to the crime scene?"

Mac had no words. Everything his wife said made perfect sense. "Have Glen and Chance left the B&B yet?"

"I'll find out right away. I have more questions for them." Brenda called Allie, who told her they were still at the inn. "Tell them to wait a minute or so. I'll be right there."

"I don't think they're in a big hurry. They're sitting in the Gathering Room talking with Holly and Luke Parker."

When Brenda walked in, the two firefighters stood up. "Allie told us you had something to ask us," Glen said. He smiled. "We want to help all we can." Brenda escorted them into her office and closed the door.

"Tell me all about your missing belt."

"I am very disappointed that I have not found it," Glen said. "It has great significance for me. The family of the children I saved that day gave it to me. They had the brass buckle engraved with my name on it. The engraving also showed a fireman holding hands with two small children."

"When did you realize it was gone?"

"The first morning I was here I decided not to wear it that day. I didn't want attention drawn to it at the firefighters convention. I'd had enough spotlight over the issue." Glen frowned. "When the convention ended, I went back to my room. I had decided to wear it for the festivities. That's when I couldn't find it. I've looked everywhere."

Brenda made notes of days and times surrounding the missing brass buckle and the belt.

"You seem very interested in the belt, Brenda," Chance said. "Do you have any idea where it is?"

Brenda hesitated. She had not discussed with Mac how to handle that question, especially since Chance had seemed certain it was the murder weapon. "I can't help you as far as locating it for you. I needed details that I failed to ask for earlier. I feel very badly for you, Glen. It sounds as if it is very special indeed." She sat back. "We will do everything to find it for you."

Chance looked intently at her. Brenda knew he was an astute man. It wasn't hard to realize he knew she had gaps in her explanation. She stood up, hoping he wouldn't press her. Glen followed suit, and Chance had no option except to do the same. Brenda remembered she had something else that needed clearing up.

"I want to ask you one more question, Glen. I noticed you and Harry seemed to share something humorous. It was noticeable because Harry seemed upbeat even though his wife had just been killed." Brenda gave specifics of the time and place where she saw them.

Glen laughed. "I do remember that. You're right, Brenda. Looking back, he did seem rather upbeat under the circumstances." Brenda raised her eyebrows to indicate she wanted his answer. "I'm sorry. He asked where I'd been the night of the festivities. He'd heard I looked very rumpled the next morning. We laughed when I told him I had become a beach bum and spent the night on the sand."

"When you were down there, did you see Harry and Colleen?"

"I saw a couple but didn't pay attention to them. They were near the area that gets rocky. I believe there was a young family closer to the water. The children wanted to see the fireworks. I remember the mother told them the fireworks were over. She reminded them that they chose to build sandcastles in the night instead of watching fireworks." He paused. "I felt relaxed and stretched out to listen to the ocean sounds. That's when I fell asleep."

Brenda thanked him for his help. She felt disappointed that he couldn't identify the couple he saw in the distance. Allie had been right. Chance and Glen didn't seem too anxious to leave the Sheffield Bed and Breakfast even though Chance had told them they needed to get back to work. When Brenda emerged from her office, Phyllis approached the two men.

"I have been searching for your missing belt, Glen. All my housekeepers are on the alert, too. I do hope we find it soon for you."

"Thank you, Phyllis. It is more than a belt. It holds great significance for me." Glen told her he was sure it would show up. Inwardly, he felt he would never see it again.

"Let's take one last walk down to the waterfront, Glen,"

Chance said. "It may be our last chance to savor the salty air."

Glen agreed. As the two men left the bed and breakfast, Brenda watched them walk across the lawn to the steps that led to the beach. They appeared to be holding a serious conversation.

"Did you lock your room every time you left it, Glen?"

"I didn't think one had to in a place like this. Sometimes I locked it, but I'm afraid I was careless about it."

Chance asked if he had secured it before they left for the closing ceremonies at the convention. Glen stated he couldn't recall. "Why do you ask? You are beginning to sound like the police."

"I think someone helped themselves to it. You mentioned to me that you thought you'd left it looped over the back of the desk chair. More than one person here admired the buckle when you wore it."

"You may be right, Chance. I suppose Brenda and Mac would need a search warrant before they could check everyone's luggage before they leave." He slowed his pace. "If someone did take it, they couldn't wear it unless they lived far away from the East Coast. Anyone who saw it would want to look at the details."

"It will show up."

Brenda called Mac. "I'm tired of walking on eggshells around Harry Sullivan. Is there anything at all you can hold him on?"

"Believe me, I've checked and rechecked his background. There is nothing to arrest him for. He has no outstanding warrants. Nothing." Brenda's response was a deep sigh.

Luke Parker took Holly's hand. "I hate to leave here, Holly. Despite what happened, this has been one of the most relaxing times I've had in a very long time."

"I agree with you, though Colleen's murder has jarred me

more than I expected. I wonder what happened to her, and why."

"She didn't appear to be a happy person. Of course, once we heard about her missing sister, that became understandable." Luke looked at his wife. "I've wondered if whoever killed her is the same person that kidnapped her sister. It all ties together."

"I hadn't thought about that," Holly said. "Melissa said Colleen had a lead on Marcy that she had been seen in this area. Maybe Marcy hadn't been seen here at all. Maybe whoever took her decided to do away with Colleen to stop her search."

Brenda overheard Holly's last remark. She joined her guests. "What you have stated could be a possibility if Colleen really had a missing sister. As it turns out, the woman she thought was her sister wasn't related at all." Brenda briefly explained Colleen's drive to find a sister she always wanted. "I think she was sincere and did believe she was on the trail to find her sister, but Marcy Scott wasn't related to her at all."

"There goes that premise," Holly said. "I do hope you find who killed her, Brenda. Colleen came across as very fragile. She didn't deserve to die like that."

Brenda smiled. She realized her existence had been tied up in the murder of Colleen Sullivan. She regretted neglecting her guests.

"I hope you have enjoyed your visit here, though I know the matter with Colleen probably upset you."

Holly and Luke assured her they loved the experience of staying in the historic Queen Anne.

"Your uncle knew what he was doing," Luke said. "We're so happy he was tenacious enough to see the restoration through."

"We'll be back, Brenda, if you'll have us," Holly said.

"Of course. You will be welcomed back any time you wish to come."

"We're thinking about coming during the wintertime. Are you open during Christmas?" Holly's eyes sparkled.

"We are open through the end of December, including Christmas and New Year's Eve. We close for two weeks beginning in January."

The Parkers decided they would return for Christmas. They were already making plans for that visit when Brenda excused herself and left for the precinct. When she got to the parking lot behind the inn, she saw Harry Sullivan packing his car. She checked with Mac, who told her he didn't want Harry to leave yet.

"Mac has asked that you hold off leaving for a few more hours, Harry." Brenda's tone of voice didn't indicate he had a choice.

"Am I under arrest for something?"

"No, but your wife was killed, and we thought you'd want to stick around to assist in finding her killer."

Brenda had no idea where those words came from. Assisting in the crime investigation had been Harry's driving force since the murder. And here she was inviting him into helping solve the case. She expected a flicker of pleasure in his eyes. Instead, she picked up suspicion. Brenda had an idea of how to lure him to where she wanted him.

"Why don't you come back to the precinct right now and ask Mac to allow you to leave? He deals better face to face than over the phone." She held her breath. Mac had no preference how he communicated when it came to solving crimes. Her ploy worked.

"All right. I'll go down there and convince him to let me leave. If he won't, then the only way he can hold me here is to arrest me. I didn't kill my wife."

Brenda assured him that he wouldn't be detained for long. "I'll be there. The detective is a fair man. He doesn't want to keep you from your job." When she saw Harry's scowl disappear, she asked if he had spoken with his in-laws.

"I haven't talked with them at all. Mac said he called them. I'm sure they are taking the news hard. I'll visit them as soon as I get back home. By the way, Colleen mentioned more than once that when she died, she opted for cremation. When will her body be released?"

"You'll have to ask Mac about that. I don't know if he has word from the coroner yet or not."

Harry drove ahead of Brenda to the police station. When they walked into Mac's office, Brenda noted the evidence box with Colleen Sullivan's name on it. The detective looked up with surprise when he saw Harry.

"Harry has a request of you. I suggested he come down and talk with you face to face. You know how you prefer that rather than over the phone." Brenda's eyes held Mac's. He got the message.

"What did you wish to ask me, Harry?"

"I'd like to leave for home. They won't keep my job waiting for me forever."

"I'm sure they understand your loss. They can't be that uncaring to give your job away."

"Detective, I'm getting restless hanging around here. I need something to do. I know you can't legally hold me unless you arrest me. Is that your plan?"

"I have no plans to arrest anyone yet. We are still gathering facts."

Harry sat forward. "How can I help you? I told you I'm good at solving cold cases." He snickered. "It's not as if I've ever managed to convince anyone associated with the law to work with me. I've seen gaps in many investigations. If I'd been listened to, some of those crimes would be solved today."

Harry Sullivan was back to his seesaw personality. Brenda wondered whether Harry or Colleen was the mentally unstable one. She began to doubt it was his wife.

CHAPTER TWELVE

Chief Bob Ingram had been on vacation. Officer Bryce Jones filled him in on the latest case.

"Are there any suspects yet?" Bob said.

The young detective told him there were two being considered. "One is the husband. The other one is a fireman who has been a guest at the Sheffield Bed and Breakfast, too."

"I'll go have a talk with Mac." The chief tapped lightly on the door. Brenda opened it for him. Chief Ingram almost voiced his questions about the recent crime before he realized a man who appeared to be in his thirties was sitting there.

Mac introduced Harry. "Unfortunately, his wife was recently murdered in Harbor Park." Mac provided brief details. "We are about to take him to one of the interrogation rooms for a more private conversation. He wishes to help us all he can."

Harry failed to hide the beam in his face. Chief Ingram realized the man wasn't too torn up over his wife's untimely death. He stood aside as Brenda, Mac, and Harry walked out. They settled across from Harry.

"Why don't we start from the beginning, Harry?" Mac suggested. "Tell us everything so we don't miss any details." He clasped his hands. "Sometimes it is the smallest element that can solve a case."

Harry sat forward. "I know it is. I'll go over it all with you again." Harry repeated his story. Brenda had felt certain he would change some of it, but he stuck to his original version.

"The biggest problem I have with it all," Brenda said, "is that the window between your time on the beach and her murder is narrow. Are you sure you went to the Octopus Tavern with people you didn't know?"

"I recall that perfectly. I was growing weary of Colleen's depressing attitude when we should have been celebrating. I needed a good stiff drink. Like I told you, I got smashed and barely made it back to the bed and breakfast. I crashed on the bed and didn't wake up until the next morning. I had no idea if Colleen returned or not. I figured she had gotten up early and gone downstairs."

An officer tapped on the door. He stepped inside and handed Mac a note. Mac flipped the message open. Lab results were back on the handprint. It dawned on him that they hadn't taken a palm print from Harry. They had fingerprints and DNA, but no handprints.

Mac relaxed. He sent a faint smile across the table. "It seems they need one more test from you if you don't mind, Harry. Since you delve into crime, I'm sure you understand the maze one must go through."

"Sure. I get it. That's something I admire in you, Detective. You get to the nitty-gritty of things, unlike some I've worked with. What can I do?"

Mac told him he could stay right where he was. He asked the officer to bring him the larger print pad. Brenda felt apprehensive that Mac planned to get more prints at the interrogation table. She felt better knowing that the chief watched from behind the one-way mirror. She was a witness as well as the officer on standby inside the door. When he returned with the necessary materials, Mac asked Harry if he minded making a handprint for him.

"No problem," Harry said. "I'll do both hands if it helps you."

"That's a good idea. Then we won't have to bother you again about it." There was no reason to have prints of both palms. Mac only needed the left one.

When the task was completed, Mac asked Harry to remain where he was. He asked Brenda to accompany him. He nodded to the officer to leave, too. Chief Ingram watched the man sitting alone. Mac and Brenda joined him.

"Officer Thompson is taking the palm print to the lab. We have results back from the evidence, but I want them matched up. If the print belongs to Harry, we have our man." Mac explained to the chief about the palm print found. "It looks as if the murderer put his hand on the ground to assist in standing back up."

During the wait, the three watched the suspect. The longer they left him alone, the more restless he became. He stood up and paced back and forth in the room before he sat down again. This movement repeated several more times. When Brenda was handed the results, she gave them to Mac.

"We have more to say to Harry Sullivan. Let's go."

Usually, a drink was offered to someone being interrogated. Neither Brenda nor Mac made the gesture.

"I'm a little thirsty," Harry said. "I wonder if I could get a bottle of water?"

The officer left to get the water. Mac read Harry Sullivan his rights. "Do you wish to have an attorney present?"

"What? Why do I need an attorney?"

"I asked if you would like one before we proceed, since I am arresting you for the murder of Colleen Sullivan."

The officer returned in time to stop Harry from standing up. "I didn't kill anyone. I certainly would never have killed my wife."

"We have evidence to the contrary," Brenda said. "Your DNA is in several places along with Colleen's at the murder scene."

Harry looked around at everyone in the little room. Then he slumped in his chair and sighed. "No attorney in the world can help me. I admit it. I did kill her. Have you ever lived with someone whose entire world is caught up in searching for a non-existent sister? Do you know how exasperating that can be, day in and day out, to put up with something you know is a lie?"

Brenda and Mac allowed him to rant for the next ten minutes. In that time, he revealed more about his actions the night he killed Colleen.

"The fireman was proud of that belt buckle. Colleen even focused on it long enough to compliment him on it. I planned it so well. I noticed Glen Adams wasn't careful about locking the door to his room. I stopped to chat with him before he closed the door. When I saw the belt looped over the back of the chair, I knew what to do. I distracted him enough that he didn't think about securing the door when he left. He wasn't expected back until noon, since they were going to the last day of the convention. Who would believe an awarded fireman would kill someone?"

"Were you and Colleen ever on the beach?" Brenda said.

"We were there. I saw Glen come down to the water. The skies had cleared from the firework display. I don't think he saw us at all. We were near the water in the rocky area. Colleen complained the pebbles were getting between her toes. She wore flip-flops. I suggested we walk downtown and mingle for a while, but, as usual, she didn't want to be in crowds. I convinced her we wouldn't walk on the main street. We chose the alley that runs behind all the specialty shops. When we got close to the park, we could hear the music playing louder. I knew exactly where we were going. It didn't take much to sway her to the outer part of Harbor Park."

Harry chuckled at his wise planning. "She agreed to find solitude at the pavilion at the back edge of the park. Everyone was dancing and having a good time. No one noticed us in the darkness. At first, we sat on the grass. She complained there was more dirt than grass and asked to move closer to the green area near the pavilion."

His eyes were like hardened steel. "That did it for me. I was sick to death of her complaints. I recall few times when her voice had a lilt in it. I suppose it was before she discovered that photo of Marcy Scott."

"What did you do next?" Brenda asked.

"I had Glen's belt rolled in a tight ball. It was stuffed in my cargo pocket. With no warning, I flipped her over face down. I held her until I had the belt ready. It didn't take long. I'm quick in my actions. She asked me what I was doing. I told her it was time for some fun." He chuckled. "I told her it was a game to see if she was strong enough to get away from me. She even laughed a little and got right into it."

Harry appeared to relish the memory. "I jerked her head up and slipped the belt around her neck and pulled with everything I had. When I saw that the buckle caught close to the side of her neck, I ignored it and pulled tighter. I saw blood coming from her ear. Then she died. My hand got smeared with some of the blood. I hefted myself up, tossed the belt where I was sure a good police force would find it. Then I went to the party where I met the men I didn't know. I was ready for a strong drink by that time."

At Mac's signal, the officer slipped handcuffs on the murderer. As he was led to a cell, he called over his shoulder. "I may be going to jail, but it's the first freedom I've felt since I married that miserable woman." They heard the cell door clang.

Mac looked at his wife. "If I ever get on your nerves that badly, Brenda, tell me. Don't kill me."

"I don't foresee that happening, but one never knows." They laughed.

"That confession didn't sound like a comedy," said Chief Ingram, who hadn't heard their bantering.

"It definitely was far from a comedy. Mac made me promise not to kill him if he got on my nerves." Brenda grew somber. "What about Glen's cherished belt and buckle?" She explained to Chief Ingram the story of the award the fireman had received.

"As soon as the trial is over, he will get it back."

"I'll be relieved when I can finally tell him the truth about his missing belt," Brenda said.

"I can't imagine he would want it back now," Mac said.

Brenda thought about it. Then she suggested he keep the buckle even if he didn't want a belt that was used to murder someone. "I know Chance has his suspicions about the way I explained my last interview with them. It will be a relief to tell them both the truth at last." She pulled at Mac's arm. "Let's go home and enjoy the guests who are still around," Brenda said.

"That's a good idea, Brenda. I know you feel badly about neglecting them these past few days."

"I'm thankful for Allie and Phyllis. They have kept things going for everyone. Most of the guests have spent more time downtown than at the bed and breakfast anyway."

Chance Rogers and Glen Adams had decided to wait around for Brenda to return. Chance vowed to get the truth from her. He had no doubt that somehow Glen's belt was involved in the murder of Colleen Sullivan. The firefighters deserved to know the truth.

They heard voices from the back entrance, and Brenda and Mac walked down the passageway. They smiled at one another before greeting Phyllis and William. Allie had left for the day. The Pendletons were determined to wait for their friends to arrive home whether they had concluded the investigation or not. Phyllis found it hard to contain herself. This was the first time that she and Brenda hadn't talked about the proceedings of crime solving as in the past.

"It's about time you two got home," Phyllis said. Brenda's eyes apologized for leaving her friend out of the loop for so long. "We want to know how the investigation is going."

"Poor Colleen," Holly said. "I do hope you have found the one who killed her."

"We have arrested someone for her murder," Brenda said. "Harry Sullivan has confessed he killed his wife. We have evidence that he did."

Hope gasped. "He killed his own wife?"

"It seems he grew exasperated over her obsession about her fake sister's disappearance," Brenda said. "According to him, he reached the point of no return. He knew she didn't have a sister. Her parents told him that when he contacted them to ask about it. The Marcy Scott she tried to find was missing and has been found but is no relation to her." Silence followed her announcement. Brenda turned to Glen Adams. "We found your belt, Glen."

Her tone of voice told the fireman he knew where it was found and what it had been used for. "I don't wish to have it back," he said. The others stared at him. "The only thing that matters is the buckle. I never want to see the belt again."

Everyone realized where the missing belt had gone and why. "Let's all go into the Gathering Room," Mac said. "I'll open the bar. Maybe Luke will play for us. Entertainment is what we all need." He looked at the jazz musician. "How much do you charge, Luke?"

"For this crowd, it's on the house." He picked up his saxophone and grinned.

ABOUT WENDY MEADOWS

Wendy Meadows is a USA Today bestselling author whose stories showcase women sleuths. To date, she has published dozens of books, which include her popular Sweetfern Harbor series, Sweet Peach Bakery series, and Alaska Cozy series, to name a few. She lives in the "Granite State" with her husband, two sons, two mini pigs and a lovable Labradoodle.

Join Wendy's newsletter to stay up-to-date with new releases. As a subscriber, you'll also get BLACKVINE MANOR, the complete series, for FREE!

Join Wendy's Newsletter Here
wendymeadows.com/cozy